THE RESTAURANT DIARIES
À LA CARTE

THE RESTAURANT DIARIES
À LA CARTE

BRANDON D. BRADLEY

BRADLEY GROUP PUBLISHING
MCDONOUGH, GA

À LA CARTE

This book is based on true events. The author has tried to recreate events, locales, and conversations from memory. To maintain anonymity, the author has changed the names of individuals and places. Some events have been slightly altered for entertainment, and some dialogue has been recreated.

À LA CARTE Copyright 2019 Brandon D. Bradley

ISBN-13: 978-1-7332237-0-6
ISBN-10: 1-7332237-0-3

Published by Bradley Group Publishing
McDonough, GA

Printed in the United States of America

First Edition July 2019
Cover Design by Make Your Mark Publishing Solutions
Interior Layout by Make Your Mark Publishing Solutions
Editing by Make Your Mark Publishing Solutions

*To my wife, Carmen, for always encouraging me to
be a better version of myself.*
&
*To my children, Camren, Cidney, Cortney,
and Brandon, all that I do is for you.
I love you all!*

ACKNOWLEDGEMENTS

This book is based on my extensive experience working in the restaurant industry from the late '80s to the present. I personally thank each person I have encountered while working at these restaurants for unknowingly giving me an infinite number of storylines, which made writing this book possible. Thank you for every experience, whether it was positive or negative, for I gained valuable lessons (or interesting stories) from each.

Thank you to my friend Melanie for encouraging me to continue writing over the years. To my brother Don, thank you for convincing me that my stories were funny, and I was sitting on a great book. Thank you, Monique with Make Your Mark Publishing Solutions for guiding me in every aspect of self-publishing. Of course, I want to thank my wife, Carmen, for allowing me to write a book about my past. I can truly say I am only thankful for my past because it led me to you!

MEET CARTER

HEY! I'M DAJAUN CARTER, BUT I GO BY CARTER. PEOPLE TEND to mess up my first name by either mispronouncing or misspelling, so I learned to make it easier on everyone. I've been working in the restaurant industry for over thirty years, and, no, I'm not 100 years old. I started working when I was fourteen, and I had no idea I'd stay for most of my adult life.

It started with a summer job. I was sick of doing chores at home for a whopping five-dollar-a-week allowance. I figured if I got a part-time job for the summer, I could make a heck of a lot more money.

That summer job turned into a lifetime of restaurant work. I discovered my passion for serving others, and I still have that passion today. Throughout the years, I've learned quite a bit about restaurants because I've done just about everything. I've swept floors, washed dishes, bussed and served tables, prepped and cooked food, trained new workers, managed crews, managed managers, and even helped open new restaurants.

While working in the industry, I've experienced things the average person wouldn't fathom. I wouldn't believe some of the stories myself if I hadn't been right there in the thick of it all. Sometimes, I sit back and reminisce on all the things I've seen, heard, and done while working at some of America's favorite restaurants. Some of this stuff is just too good to keep to myself, so I thought I'd share the best and worst moments, the shocking and unbelievable, the hilarious and downright sad.

Welcome to *The Restaurant Diaries.*

WHAT IS THIS IN MY ICE CREAM?

I GOT MY FIRST JOB IN 1987, AT A WELL-KNOWN ICE CREAM PARLOR (who even says parlor these days). My manager trained me, going over food waste and the proper way to scoop the ice cream. Now, for the customer, it seemed they were getting a beautiful, perfectly scooped serving of ice cream, but for the business, it was imperative to not give any extra. To scoop ice cream, it was important to use three essential tools: the scraper, scooper, and warm water. The scraper served two purposes: to prevent you from pulling a muscle in your arm while scooping and to scrape all the ice cream off the walls of the container to get every single morsel. Everyone has used a scooper and knows what it's for, but the water may be the most important part. Without dipping the scooper into the warm water, you cannot get perfectly rounded scoops of ice cream, and you may also lose a lot of ice cream due to it sticking to the scooper.

My manager reiterated that we did not waste product. I listened with intent because I wanted to make the same amount of money he was making. I was only making $3.35 per hour. This guy was making a whopping $4.50 per hour. He knew he was the big dog, making the big bucks. He acted like Louie Anderson's character in the movie *Coming to America*: *"Hey, I started out mopping the floor like you guys. But now, I'm washing lettuce. Soon, I'll be on fries, then the grill. In a year or two, I'll make assistant manager, and that's when the big bucks start rolling in."* Although he was cocky, I paid close attention. I knew that in a year or two, I could be making $4.50 per hour.

Well, my desire to be like him ceased almost immediately. As he demonstrated the perfect scooping technique, he accidentally dropped the ice cream on the floor. I didn't judge him. I knew everyone made mistakes, even at his high level. But I was disgusted when he scooped the ice cream off the floor and put it back into the container—every bit of it. Even though I was only fourteen, I knew that was taboo.

"Soooo, you're just gonna pick that ice cream up off the floor and put it back in there?" I asked.

He looked at me, poking his finger into my chest, and said, "We waste *nothing*."

He repeated the motto and I nodded. "We waste nothing," I echoed. I knew it was wrong but, at fourteen, what was I going to do?

Later, a customer came in and ordered that same ice cream he had dropped on the floor. I tried to offer her another flavor, but he jumped in and told her it was a nice selection. As he scooped the ice cream, he glared at me, daring me to say something. I kept my mouth shut.

The lady started eating her ice cream right away but stopped. She looked at him and asked, "What is this in my ice cream?"

I walked away.

Run, Don't Jog

THE AREA WHERE THE PARLOR WAS LOCATED HAD A BAD problem with people using fake money or trying to trick the cashiers. People would often tell us they'd paid with a twenty-dollar bill, but they'd really paid with a ten. We were taught to not put the money inside the register until we had given the customers their change. There were also quick change artists, who would wait for us to tell them the total amount due and try to confuse us. If their bill was $3.63, they would give the cashier a five-dollar bill, but when they received their change of $1.37, they would say, "Oh no, I meant to pay with this ten-dollar bill because I need change." They would try to get us to give them back the five-dollar bill and have us give them the change for the ten dollars as well. So now, we've given them back the $1.37 change, the five-dollar bill, and the change from the ten dollars. This was too confusing for a fourteen-year-old boy handling money for the first time.

People ran scams like that often, but I was only scammed once. After that, I vowed it would never happen to me again. When they tried to do a quick change after I had given them change, I simply wouldn't do it. If they needed change, I broke down the amount they needed, but I was never involved in another quick change scam again.

One day, a customer came in and paid for his order with a roll of quarters. I didn't think anything of it at first. We needed the quarters. As soon as he walked out, I broke open the roll and discovered I had been scammed. He had put a roll of pennies inside but had placed a quarter at each end, making it appear as if it was a whole roll of quarters. I was furious and, at fourteen years of age, full of testosterone. I thought I was the toughest guy in the world. When I told the young lady with whom I was working what happened, she got me hyped up and told me to go catch the guy. Without thinking, I went right out the door and started yelling at him.

He wouldn't turn around, so I went after him. I didn't know if the guy was deaf or not because he wouldn't turn around. Other people on the street were looking at him and me, but no one wanted to get involved. He started jogging as I got closer to him, so I knew he'd heard me. He slipped into the alley behind one of the stores. As I entered the alley behind him, he turned around and slid a knife out of his pocket. That was when I realized I was chasing a grown-ass man, and I was just a little boy.

He looked at me, smiling, with the knife in his hand. "You sure you want to come get this money from me?" he asked.

Embarrassed and afraid, I shook my head.

He slowly walked toward me, and I backed up at the same pace.

"Come on, tough guy! Come get this money from me," he said, taunting me.

I was glad I still had on my apron and I'd worn dark jeans because I had to stop myself from peeing my pants. I stared at him pleadingly, trying to hold back tears of fear. "No, sir. I don't want the money back. I'm sorry for chasing you."

"Bring your little ass here, boy."

I didn't move. I looked at him and back at the knife. I could see the sunlight glistening off the blade. I held my breath. He was grinning at me, like this was a game, enjoying my fear as he watched me stare at the knife.

He calmly folded the knife and slid it back into his pocket. "See, I put the knife away. I'm not going to hurt you. Now, come here, and let me talk to you."

I didn't know what kind of sick thoughts were plaguing his mind, but I had to get out of there.

He started toward me. I turned around and ran back toward the restaurant, feeling stupid.

When I got back to the ice cream shop, my coworker smiled with excitement. "Did you catch him?" she asked. "You were gone for a while."

I tried to sound brave as the lie rolled easily from my lips. "Naw, I didn't catch him. I almost caught him, but he jumped into a car as I got closer. I started yanking on the door, but he sped off. He was scared, though."

She soaked up every word of my shameless lie, egging me on. "I bet we won't ever see him again!"

I prayed that was true.

I excused myself and went to the bathroom. As soon as I got inside, I checked my underwear. *Whew! No mistake!*

I never told my manager about the incident. I would've likely been fired and never made that $4.50 per hour I desperately wanted. He probably would've broken out the rules and regulations handbook and went over it with me before firing me. If he had, I would've asked him to show me the part that explains picking ice cream up off the floor. You would've thought the guy owned the place, but I know where he got his behavior from—the owners!

Big Shirley

THE OWNERS SAT IN THEIR MINIVAN ACROSS THE STREET FROM THE parlor, just watching the place. I guess they didn't realize, just as clearly as they could see us, we could see them, but I don't think they cared. That was probably what they wanted. Their daughter worked at both their locations as the store manager. She reminded me of Shirley from the hit '70s TV show *What's Happening?* She was bigger and meaner than Shirley, though, so I referred to her as *Big* Shirley. Just like her parents, she was tough as nails and would say anything that was on her mind.

The first time I worked at night, she told me to mop the floors. Although I had come from a strict household, where my mom kept our place spotless, I had never mopped a day in my life.

I told her I had never mopped before, and Big Shirley had a fit. She started mouthing off. "What kind of house did you grow up in that you've never mopped before? What does your mom do? She should be ashamed of herself!"

Although Big Shirley was *big*, I had a problem with her talking about my mama. My mom did a great job and had raised us right. I looked at her sideways, but Big Shirley didn't care. She would've whooped me something nice, but it still wouldn't have mattered. Nobody talked about my mama!

I grabbed the mop and began what I thought was mopping. There was already some grayish water in the bucket, so I took the mop out, put it on the floor, and started moving it around. I didn't know Big Shirley could move that fast. All I heard was big stomps coming toward me. For a moment, I thought I was in a *Godzilla* movie.

She screamed, "What are you doing?!"

"I'm mopping the floor!"

She snatched the mop from me. "That is *not* how you do it."

She pointed at me and told me to follow her. She showed me the procedure for properly mopping the floor. She went through every motion without taking her eyes off me or saying a word, all with a scowl on her face. She first swept the floor—and I mean she swept every nook and cranny—and put it all into the dustpan. She took the bucket to the sink and poured out all the dirty water (still looking at me). She rinsed out the bucket (eyes still on me). Next, she cleaned off the dirty mophead with clean water and wrung out the mophead without taking her eyes off me. Part of me felt as if she were daydreaming about wringing my neck. She added soap and hot water to the bucket (still watching me).

Finally, Big Shirley began mopping the floor. She started at the front door and worked her way backward through the entire parlor. She continued to re-dip the mophead and wring it out. She kept her eyes locked on me through the entire process as if she were daring me to look away. And I didn't dare.

Once she was done, she finally spoke to me. "Now *that* is how you mop!"

I had to admit the floors looked great. Internally, I smiled and snickered. She'd wanted me to do the floors, but she ended up doing it. Haha!

As if she knew what I was thinking, she took the mop bucket and mop and rolled it back to the front of the parlor. *No way is this lady about to do that again!* I thought.

She was making the floors bad again because she was walking through her work, streaking the freshly mopped floor with soiled footprints and wheel marks from the bucket. She pointed at me and gestured for me to come to her. I walked through the floor, making my own marks. She handed me the mop and, much to my surprise, kicked the bucket over, causing the dirty water to spill all over the floor.

She said, "Now *you* do it!" while glowering at me.

She watched me do the entire process without taking her eyes off me. I could see her looking, but I didn't dare look at her. The lady was a monster, but I sure did mop that floor like I was an expert.

After we had mopped the entire parlor, she told me to take out all the trash. Cool, I had taken the trash out before. I did it at home all the time. I even had to take the trash outside and put it in the alley behind the garage at home, so this was a piece of cake. She left me alone to do that. I took the trash from the little trash can in their office and put it inside the bigger trash can next to the back door. We had already taken out the trash from the front before we mopped the floors. It was already inside the bigger trash can, so I took the bag out of the trash can and went outside to take the trash out. I tossed it into the large dumpster and attempted to go back into the building. The door was locked.

I knocked on the door, but no one opened it. I kept knocking but, apparently, I was being ignored. I had to walk back to the front of the building to try to get Big Shirly to let me in. I started banging on the front door, but she wouldn't answer. I knew she could see me because there was a two-way mirror at the front of the restaurant. The customers thought it was a regular mirror, but the owners and Big Shirley used the two-way mirror to see into the lobby and watch their employees.

I saw Big Shirley pop her head up from the back. She yelled, "We are closed!"

"It's me!" I shouted back.

She squinted. "Go around to the back."

I squinted, too, and I wanted to give her the finger, but I walked back around to the back door of the parlor, thinking she would be there waiting for me, but she was not. I had to knock on the back door.

"Who is it?" she yelled.

"Who do you think?"

She swung the door open, looking like a giant as she stared down at me. She said, "Young man, don't ever get smart with me."

I walked in, and she hurriedly closed the door. She yelled at me for going outside without telling anyone. "There should always be somebody at the door when we're taking the trash out for safety reasons. The back door self-locks when it closes. She looked around. "Why didn't you take all the trash out?"

I scanned the parlor and saw there was no more trash in sight. "I *did* take all the trash out."

"Did you take the containers out of the freezer and throw those away?"

"No, I haven't been inside the freezer."

"You need to go into the freezer and take the empty containers out. The empty containers are trash and should be taken out daily."

A big black coat with a furry hood hung on the outside of the freezer. Dried ice cream stains covered it. Big Shirley pointed at it and instructed me to put it on before going into the freezer. I looked hesitantly at the oversized coat because I didn't want to put it on.

As if Big Shirley had read my mind again, she opened the freezer and said, "Fine, don't put it on, but you have to get those empty containers off the floor and get them outside in the trash."

It was already ten thirty at night, and I was ready to go home. The faster I completed the task, the faster I could leave. I walked into the freezer, thinking I could do it quickly and avoid having to put that dirty coat on. It only took me about three seconds to realize that was a mistake. This was the biggest freezer I had ever seen. I had never been inside a walk-in freezer. It had to be fifteen feet long, with containers of ice cream everywhere. I had built up a sweat from mopping and taking the trash out, and the cold air hit me immediately. I had never been to Antarctica before, but this had to be what it felt like. I was instantly aware of every morsel of sweat on my body because they each turned into ice crystals on my skin.

Big Shirley was still holding the door to the freezer with one hand, and she held the jacket out for me with the other. "Would you like the jacket now, genius?"

Without saying a word, I put the jacket on.

"There are gloves inside the pocket, genius boy." She showed me the temperature gauge located on the outside of the freezer. "The temperature inside the freezer must always be maintained between zero and negative ten degrees to keep the ice cream frozen."

The coat reeked. It must've absorbed dried up, frozen sweat and ice cream from every employee who had ever worked there.

While I was inside, getting boxes from the back, the freezer door slammed shut. My heart dropped. I dashed toward the door and panicked when I discovered there was no door handle. This was it! I knew my parents would find me frozen to death in this big freezer. What a sad way to die. All kinds of thoughts plagued my mind. *Big Shirley did this on purpose. She's going to freeze me and eat me!* I wondered how many other people she had frozen and why the police didn't know about it.

Okay Carter, start praying! I closed my eyes and said the Lord's Prayer. Surely, if God saved Daniel from the lions' den and helped David beat Goliath, He could help me. I kept praying, but nothing happened. I was seconds away from crying but feared the tears would freeze as they fell.

I started jogging in place, puffing out clouds of cold air as I felt every organ in my body began to freeze. This was the end! I wasn't going to make it. I knew death was near, but I refused to give up. I banged on the door for a short eternity, screaming for another chance at life. "Hey! Let me out! Let me out, please! I don't wanna die, not like this, not today! Please let me out!"

Finally, Big Shirley opened the door. I ran out, with a cold rush of air behind me.

"What are you doing all that screaming for?" she scolded.

"I was locked in the freezer. I thought I was going to die!"

She scowled at me, disgusted. "How were you going to die?"

"I was in there for almost an hour, and you wouldn't let me out!"

Big Shirley folder her arms. "Little boy, you weren't in there for no damn hour, and why didn't you just come out?"

I knew she was lying. I looked at the clock to confirm and call her out. Shockingly, it said 10:32. I had been in the freezer for less than two minutes. "I tried to push it open, and I even banged on the door, but it still wouldn't open," I explained.

She shook her head and walked into the freezer without the coat. I figured her polar-bear-like blubber would protect her from the cold. The door closed behind her. After about ten seconds, she came out with empty ice cream containers. She looked at me and shook her head. "Genius boy, you can't get locked in the freezer."

"But there's no handle!"

She showed me a small wheel attachment on the freezer door. I had attempted to turn it while I was dying, but it didn't budge. "I think it's frozen into place," I said. She must've been incredibly strong to turn that thing because I had tried with all my strength.

"You must really be a genius boy." She pushed the wheel in with ease. "As a safety protocol, no one can get locked into this type of freezer. When the door closes, all you have to do is push the dial with the palm of your hand, and the door opens."

I was relieved to know how to open the door, but I was even more thankful that she wasn't trying to freeze me to death and come back later to thaw and cook me.

I took all the empty containers out of the freezer and lined them up by the back door. There must've been about twenty boxes. Big Shirley stood by the door as I took them out. She told me to put the containers in the first dumpster because it was for boxes only.

"Oh," I said. "I put the trash bag in that one." I tried to stop myself, but she had already heard me.

"You didn't notice the wording on the side that says, 'boxes only'? You need to climb in there and get that bag out."

"What?!"

"You heard me! You need to get in that dumpster and get that bag out of there."

Filled with anger, I climbed into the dumpster, pulled the trash out, and tossed it into the other dumpster. After I climbed out, I started tossing the empty containers into the correct dumpster. The whole time, Big Shirley stood at the door, working on a crossword puzzle. Someone could've snuck up on us and robbed the ice cream shop if they wanted to because she wasn't paying attention. Then again, I don't think anyone would've had the courage to sneak up on Big Shirley.

"Okay, I'm done," I said.

She looked at the dumpster, unimpressed. "You needed to break the boxes down first."

"What do you mean 'break the boxes down'?"

"You should've stepped on them before you put them into the dumpster. We need to flatten the boxes, so we can get more in the dumpster." She had stood there the entire time while I threw those boxes in here. She could've told me that to start. "Well, you need to get back in there and stomp those boxes down."

Huffing, I climbed into the dumpster and jumped on the empty boxes, each one splattered with thawed ice cream. My shoes and pants were soiled and disgusting, but I was glad I didn't step on a rat or something. I climbed out and asked, "Anything else?"

"Nah!" she replied as she went back to doing her crossword puzzle. "You can go home, but get your things and go out the back door. I'm not letting you walk through the front with your nasty shoes."

I shook my head. I didn't know about this new job. All this for $3.35?

My dad was waiting for me in the car. He smiled at me and said, "Look at my hard-working son. I'm proud of you!"

As we walked into the house, my mom asked, "How was work?"

"Fine," I replied as I went to my room to take off my dirty clothes. I didn't dare tell her what Big Shirley had said about her. However, I had a new appreciation for my mother and all the steps she took to keep our house clean.

PIZZA PIZZA

I WORKED AT THE ICE CREAM PARLOR OFF AND ON FOR TWO summers. The more I worked with Big Shirley and the owners, the more I resented the place. They never had anything positive to say, and they were always in a bad mood. I was also sick of jumping into dumpsters. I never saw a rat, but I couldn't stand the thought of being surrounded by trash. My measly pay never increased much, and I couldn't find the value in working there. The pay didn't match the work, so I decided my ice cream days were over.

My second job, and my favorite, was at a pizza place. I always wanted to work there. My oldest brother used to work there before he went off to college, and my other brother was still there. He'd gotten me the job. I loved it right away. My brother showed me around on the first day. We got to what looked like another walk-in freezer, and I just about panicked. Holding my breath, we walked inside, but it was just a cooler. The temperature was cold, but my brother explained that it stayed between thirty-six and forty degrees in there. I could manage that.

My brother was the assistant manager, and the store manager

was a lady named Mrs. Ellen. Everyone followed Mrs. Ellen's directions. She ran the restaurant as if she owned it.

Shortly after I was hired, the place was robbed. Unfortunately, when it happened, both my brother and Mrs. Ellen were working. I was lucky because I had just left for the day. My brother said they were robbed about ten minutes after I had walked out the door.

Two guys waited until the lobby was clear before they made their move. They were being indecisive about what they wanted to order when one of the guys pretended to accidentally drop his bottle of pop.

"Oh, I'm so sorry," he said.

"We can help clean up the mess if you need us," his friend added."Don't worry about it," Mrs. Ellen reassured them. "One of the employees will take care of it." She gestured to my brother, instructing him to clean up the mess.

The two guys left, and my brother unlocked the door behind the counter and started walking into the lobby, providing the opportunity they'd been waiting for. They rushed back inside, this time, wielding a gun instead of a pop bottle.

One of them pointed the gun at my brother as he walked him back toward the unlocked door. The other guy quickly locked the front door to the pizzeria. They escorted my brother and Mrs. Ellen to the back of the restaurant. Once they were out of view from the front of the store, one of the gunmen pointed his gun at Mrs. Ellen. "Take me to the safe!" he commanded.

As always, Mrs. Ellen acted like she owned the restaurant. She could've been keeping her personal life savings at the restaurant because she didn't want to tell the robber where the safe was. "Safe? What do you mean?" she asked in an innocent tone.

The gunman repeated, "Where is the safe?!"

She shrugged. "What safe?"

"I'm not going to keep asking you where the safe is!"

Unmoved by his threats, Mrs. Ellen kept up the façade, pretending to be clueless.

After asking her three times and getting the same answer, the gunman hit her on top of her head with the butt of the gun.

"Oh, that safe!" she said.

My brother admitted he almost burst into laughter when she'd finally given in.

Mrs. Ellen survived and so did my brother. We didn't know why she was so adamant about protecting that money. It wasn't worth her life.

That was the second time my brother was involved with a robbery while working there. When it happened again, he was helping out at another location that had a drive-thru. This was one of the first pizza places to add a drive-thru. Although it was a good idea for business, the design for the pizza pickup windows was not well thought out. With huge windows that opened wide, the workers had to stretch half their upper bodies through the opening to hand the pizza to the customers.

A group of guys pulled up to the drive-thru in a van. My brother didn't have to stretch himself far to give them their food because the van sat up higher, at the same level as the window. As he passed the pizza to the customer, the customer grabbed the window with one hand and pointed a gun at the window with the other. Instinctively, my brother let go of the pizza and jumped out of the gunman's view.

My brother's scream alerted the rest of the workers. They all watched in shock as the driver of the van started climbing through the window. One of the workers was taking a hot pizza out of the oven. When he saw the gunman, he threw it at him. My brother and his coworkers fled through the front door and ran across the street to the gas station, waiting for the police. The robbers were gone before the police arrived.

• • •

I loved working with my brother because he kept me laughing. One day, I drove to work in a snow storm. When I parked, the car got stuck in an embankment of snow. I tried to gun the engine as hard as I could, but the wheels continued to spin in one spot.

I went into the restaurant and told my brother I couldn't get the car out of the embankment.

He said, "You'll have to get back in the car and rock back and forth."

I got into the car and pushed down on the gas pedal as I rocked myself violently back and forth, thinking my movement would get the car to jolt out of the spot. Although it was bone-chilling cold outside, I was sweating profusely inside my car.

After a few minutes, my brother came outside and saw me rocking. He started laughing and asked, "What are you doing?"

Exhausted, I continued to rock. "I'm rocking the car back and forth, but it's not working."

My brother opened the car door. "Scoot over." Laughing, he got into the driver's seat and started shifting the gears gently from reverse to drive, while pressing the gas. Finally, the car was freed from the embankment, and he parked it for me. "*That* is what rocking the car means."

• • •

After my brother left to get a better job at the steel plant, we went through several managers at the pizza place over the next few months. Mrs. Ellen had left after the robbery. After a few months, they finally found a manager who would stay for about a year. His name was James. James was in his forties and had a pretty wife and two high school daughters. He was cool with most of his employees, especially the ladies.

When James got mad, he cussed a lot. It was funny because I had never heard anyone cuss as much as Richard Pryor. James would get mad at the customers at the drop of a dime, and he liked using the word "nigga." He often used that term when talking to us about a customer. "That nigga want extra pep-peroni," and "That nigga trippin'," or "That nigga gonna make me slap the shit out of him!" "Shit" was his other favorite word.

James's wife wasn't just pretty; the lady was flat-out gorgeous, and she had a professional and kind demeanor. I wondered what the heck she was doing with him. Never a day went by when James wouldn't hit on one of the female customers, and he would often get their phone numbers. He spent a lot of time on the phone at work. Back in those days, there were no cell phones, so we had to write the numbers down. James had a black book that he kept at the restaurant and never took home with him. He was safe because, although his wife came up there at least once a week to either drop off something or pick it up, she never went past the lobby. Often, when James and I closed together, he would have me do everything while he claimed to be in the back doing paperwork. But I knew he was sitting on the phone, talking to one of his lady friends, not his wife. It didn't bother me at all, though. James was lenient with me and let me do whatever I wanted.

I did learn some pointers from James, however. I listened to how he smooth talked the ladies and noticed how he didn't pay extra attention to the really pretty ones. I saw how this worked. The pretty ones were used to getting a lot of attention, so James barely gave them any. It drove them crazy, and they were always coming after him.

I started using that technique, and it worked. I worked with him one night, and it was about ten minutes before closing. James was in the back "doing paperwork," and I was up front, taking orders for the last-minute stragglers that walked in. A fine girl walked in and, this time, I couldn't be cool. She was light-skinned, just like I liked them. As one of my good friends would often say, she was a redbone. He always teased me because he thought I only liked redbone girls.

She came in by herself and ordered a slice of pizza. I asked for her name. She told me, and I could see that she was flirting back. I tried to sweet talk her through the window, but this pizza place was in Detroit, and all the fast food restaurants in the city (excluding McDonald's) had bullet-proof glass at the counters to ensure the employees didn't get shot. The underside of the counters was reinforced by steel, in case someone tried to shoot through the counter. To give customers their pizza, we had to slide it through a thin space in the bullet-proof glass that was adjoined to the counter. After sliding the pizza through, the other end wouldn't open until the first end closed. Soft drinks or smaller bags fit into the bullet-proof turnstile. To pay, the customers had to put their money in the tray slot, a space about an inch in depth, that was cut into the counter. The only things that fit were bills and coins.

I was about to go get her pizza slice, when she asked, "Can I pay you for it now?"

"Sure," I said.

She slid me five dollars through the money tray. I let the money sit there while I went to get the pizza. We were trained to never finalize the transaction until the order was complete and we had shown the customers their money. We also left the money out while we gave change, so the customer couldn't say we'd given them the wrong amount.

She stopped me as I was walking away and started flirting with me more, telling me how handsome I was. She started asking for more things: an order of breadsticks, another slice of pizza, and a soda. I was gullible, so I said, "Sure." She could've had whatever she wanted because I was convinced she was about to be my new girlfriend.

I went back to the oven to get the additional items and hurried back. When I got back, she was still there but with her head down on the counter. I asked her, "What's wrong?" I was concerned about my future girlfriend.

She looked up, crying crocodile tears. "My hand!"

I looked down at her hand and saw that it was stuck in the money tray. This chick had tried to steal her money back while I was in the back, getting her food. I didn't understand. I would've given her whatever she wanted.

After hearing the commotion, James walked in from the back to ask what was going on. He saw her hand and said, "Aw shit!"

I could tell she was in a lot of pain, but I was pissed off at her for trying to scam and use me. Now, I was the one in tears but from laughter. She screamed for me to help her. I tried to gently push her hand back through, but every time I pushed, she screamed, "Ouch!"

James walked away. "Shhiiiittt!" he mumbled under his breath.

Through my laughter, I managed to tell James I needed help. He came back and poured olive oil all over her hand, and I was able to slide her hand out. She ran out without her pizza and her five dollars.

I was still laughing as she left. James said, "You can keep that shit."

"What?"

"The five dollars and her pizza."

• • •

Although James had a gorgeous wife and a slew of women always coming to see him, it wasn't enough for him. He flirted with the young girls who worked there. At first, I thought he was just playing with them, but then I started to see some of them hanging around in the back with him. One of the girls went to high school with me. I had never seen anything like that before, a girl fooling around with someone old enough to be her daddy. I had seen it on television, but not in real life. I knew it was a problem, but I wanted nothing to do with the situation. The young lady's mom liked James, too. She would come in and flirt with him when she dropped off her daughter. But James had no interest in her. He just wanted to become cool with the mom and even flirt with her a little so he could get closer to the daughter. He was building trust with the mom, and it worked. Often, the young lady would call her mom and tell her it was going to be a late night, and she would call her back when she was close to getting off work.

Her mom would normally pick her up after we closed and wait outside in her car in front of the store. But on nights when she and James wanted to spend time together, she called her mom so she wouldn't get there early. The mom suspected nothing because she trusted James. James would tell the other workers and me he would finish up and we could go ahead and leave early. We were all happy to leave early without doing most of the cleaning, so we thought nothing of it. But he was just trying to get us out so he could fool around with the young high school girl. He had built up enough trust with the mom that, eventually, he started taking her home.

"Mom, you don't have to pick me up today," she'd tell her mom. "I should be off work in about an hour. Your friend James is getting off at the same time, and he said he can drop me off." As soon as she hung up the phone, she and James would walk out the door.

We all thought James was cool, but he wasn't cool at all. He was a pedophile. That young lady was in the tenth grade!

• • •

The pizza place was in a rough area of Detroit. That's probably why people like Mrs. Ellen and James were chosen to work there. Corporate figured they were tough enough to handle the danger. James was no fool. He wasn't going to get caught slippin'. He came to work every day with his gun, no exception. "Shhiiiittt, I'm not the one to ever get robbed. Some muthafucka come in here to rob us, they gone catch a bullet!" he warned.

And I knew James meant it. Every night, like clockwork, when we turned off the lights, locked the door, and set the alarm as we were about to leave, James cocked his gun. When we walked out the door, he always had his pistol ready, hidden beneath his jacket, which was folded on his arm.

I was never mad at him. The neighborhood was rough, and I had seen my fair share of mishaps at the job. A group of guys came into the place every Friday and Saturday night. They'd bring their boombox, play music in the lobby, and dance. They treated the restaurant like their hangout. As a matter of fact, it was. James always said something to them, but they laughed at him and turned the music up louder as if they wanted us to come from behind the counter and confront them. But even James was smart enough not to fall into their trap.

After a couple of months of the same thing, James was finally able to get them to stop coming in, but it only got worse. They started standing at the back of the restaurant and jumping on the customers, taking their pizza. The customers frantically ran back into the restaurant and reported the assault, but the guys never took anything except their pizza. This happened every week for a while until enough people reported it and the cops started rolling through. The cops would even park in front of the restaurant on some weekends, just so people could see their presence.

On several occasions, I'd seen our customers getting robbed right in the lobby. I was working oven when I witnessed the first robbery. Working oven meant I took the pizza out of the oven, sliced it, and boxed it, and I had to be fast. On the weekend, pizzas came out of the oven every thirty seconds to a minute. And all eyes were on me. The customers stared at me, hoping their pizza was next. Sometimes, they asked if they could see the pizza before I boxed it. I hated when they did that because it slowed my progress, and I knew, at any moment, another pizza would be coming out of the oven. I hated when someone stopped me and then a pizza ended up falling out of the oven. I rarely made eye contact with the customers so I could keep moving.

One night, however, it wasn't as busy as normal. I was doing my thing, taking pizzas out and slicing them, when I saw a customer walk up to the counter. While he was waiting on the cashier, two other men walked up behind him. I saw the man jerk forward like someone was pressing something into his back. Two gentlemen slid beside him. Instantly, the customer looked straight ahead. He slowly took off his watch, then his bracelet, followed by his wallet. I knew he was getting robbed. I tried to tell the girl on the phone taking orders to call the police. But she couldn't hear that well. I was talking out of the side of my mouth, but I wasn't speaking too clearly.

I tried to remain calm as if I didn't notice anything, but she kept yelling, "Call who?"

I said again, calmly and quietly, "Please call the police."

"Who? Did you say call the *police?*"

A few more people had come into the lobby. The robbers were so close to their victim that, at first glance, nothing seemed out of the ordinary. But everyone in the lobby had heard her, including the robbers. It must've spooked them because they grabbed his bracelet, wallet, and watch and took off.

The next time, I had a perfect view of a potential robbery. It was a weekday and business was slow. Four people were in the lobby, waiting to either order or pick up their food. Only James and I were working, and it was slow enough for us to split the duties. James was working the counter, taking the orders and running the cash register and drink station. I was making all the pizzas, slicing and boxing them. From where I stood, I could see the lobby and outside into the parking lot. A woman was sitting in her car in the passenger seat. A man wearing a red ski mask ran up to the car and began opening the door. Immediately, the passenger moved into the driver seat, exited through the driver side door, and ran toward our building. The carjacker jumped into the driver seat. Once he realized there were no keys in the car, he got out and ran toward our building as well. James, the customers in the lobby, and I all watched it unfold.

A door in the lobby led to the area behind the counter, where we were. It was steel enforced and remained deadbolted and locked. James ran to the door and swung it open. All the customers in the lobby and the lady who had run out of the car came swarming in behind the counter. James managed to lock the door as soon as the carjacker ran inside. He carried the largest gun I had ever seen in my life, some type of semi-automatic he had to carry with two hands. James and the customers ducked behind the counter, but for some reason, probably shock, I just stood there frozen, eye to ski mask with the gunman. He stood there for a second and just shook his head. He ran out of the building and down the street. James opened the door, and the customers ran out to their cars, forgetting about the pizza they'd just bought.

• • •

I'm always nice to the people who handle my food. I never know what kind of day they're having or what kind of person they are. I would never think about doing something to anyone's food. It doesn't matter how mean or difficult the customer is. I would simply prefer not to serve them than to do something that could potentially harm them. I found out quickly that everyone isn't cut from the same cloth. James was one of those people who couldn't care less about a customer's food. If a customer was difficult or asked too many questions, James would find a way to drop the food on the floor or step on it. I'd seen him step on the pizza dough before flattening it out.

If the customer was downright demeaning to James, he took an extra step. Not only would he step on the uncooked pizza dough, but after he prepped the pizza, before it went into the oven, he hocked and chucked a big gob of spit onto the pizza. It gave him joy to serve the special order. He'd say, "I gave you extra sauce on your pizza for your troubles!" with a big smile.

It was the most disgusting thing I had ever seen.

Taking Advantage

I WORKED FOR THE SAME COMPANY WHEN I WENT TO COLLEGE in Georgia. Because I had experience and knew how to do everything in the restaurant, after two weeks, I was promoted to assistant manager. I had the keys to the place and everything. It had been a while since I'd worked for another manager besides James. I didn't realize how much James actually worked until I came to the South.

These were some of the laziest managers I had ever worked for. One manager was obese and always sitting down. All the employees were friends. I was the outsider, and they made sure I knew it. Four people usually worked during lunch, when I came in. Within an hour, everyone left, leaving me by myself to do everything. Although they had prepped for me in the morning, the work was still too much for one person to handle. I rang in the orders, took phone orders, made the pizza, cut the pizza, cashed out the customers, and still had to clean the entire place before I left. Occasionally, another person would close with me, but that wasn't common.

The closing process was detailed at this location. I had closed the restaurant plenty of times in Detroit, but it wasn't as tedious. We had to wipe down all the counters, wash the dishes, put up the food, and cover everything with plastic wrap, which was normal protocol. But here, we were to also pay special attention to the pizza prep station. We couldn't leave out a crumb of food because the place was infested with roaches like I had never seen before. I had seen roaches from time to time while living up North but nothing like this. And these roaches were huge! They called the bigger roaches "water bugs." I'd seen water bugs before, and these were not the same. They were nothing but *big* roaches. The other employees were used to seeing them, so they never made a huge fuss about them, but I freaked out, especially when one fell from the ceiling and almost landed on the pizza station.

I had watched it the entire time, from when I first saw it climbing the wall until it was just over my head. This wasn't the roach's first attempt. It seemed to purposely align itself over the pizza station before falling. Luckily, it missed, but I remained on the lookout. From that moment, I decided I never wanted mushrooms on my pizza. I couldn't be sure they weren't baked roaches instead.

We didn't see them much during the shift, but when we opened in the morning, roaches scattered into every direction. It made me sick to my stomach. I couldn't believe a restaurant would have that type of problem. I should've known, however, because prior to my employment, they didn't do a good job cleaning the place. The main manager worked days only, and she was too fat to do anything besides sit in a chair, count money, and eat pizza. They had been sticking newer people on the night shift with no direction for years. And they wondered why they had roaches. I don't think they cared, though.

I was sure not to bring any personal items into the restaurant. I didn't want any roaches traveling home with me. As soon as I got back to my apartment, I stripped down to my shorts and shook out my clothes to be on the safe side.

I often complained about the lack of assistance on my shifts, but it never changed a thing. One night, I'd had enough. I was tired of management and my coworkers taking advantage of me. Before leaving, I told my manager and her crew I needed help, and they couldn't keep overworking me.

She said, "You'll be all right. You can handle it."

Within an hour, four of the employees ended their shifts for the day and walked out together. They talked and laughed and were having a good time as they sauntered out, carefree. I was fuming, but I knew I could handle it. Well ... I thought I could, anyway.

It was a busy night. I moved quickly, trying to work all the stations, but the customers were getting upset because everything was taking too long. Throughout the night, I could hear the customers speaking amongst themselves. "They need to get that young man some help back there. This doesn't make any sense."

This went on the entire night. Usually, I had time to start breaking some things down and cleaning. But that night, I was just too busy to do it. I knew I was going to be there all night, trying to clean. I tried to wrap up the items first, but it was like the roaches were having a family reunion. They were everywhere!

Enough is enough! I thought. *They don't want to give me any help, so I can't do this job anymore.* I grabbed my things and left. I didn't wrap up a thing, but I did turn off the lights. I wanted the roaches to go at it. I was done. I didn't count or drop the money. I locked the front door and walked out. Those bitches had some work to do the next morning.

The next day, the managers left me a few hostile messages on my voicemail. They said they had to throw away all the food I'd left out uncovered because it was contaminated. They also couldn't believe I had left without making sure the money was counted and dropped. I chuckled as I listened to the messages. Later that evening, I went by to drop off the keys. I couldn't believe it. It was after five p.m., and the whole crew was working. I handed the manager my keys to the restaurant and left. She looked like she could've punched me, which made me laugh.

I told myself I would never work at another restaurant a day in my life!

Over the next couple of years, while still in college, I went back to Detroit for summer vacation and worked odd jobs. I worked at the airport, washing cars, and I loved it, but I was exhausted at the end of the day. Customers dropped off their cars, and we were responsible for vacuuming, cleaning the windows, checking oil levels and power steering fluid, and filling the tank with gas. I worked midnights often, and the shift was great for me. Many of the cars weren't turned in during the night shift, so I could pace myself. Usually, during the last two hours, I slept in a car, waiting for my shift to end.

I worked at a steel plant the next summer. They were only hiring college students whose parents worked at the plant. My mom was a nurse there, and my brother worked there as well. The money was great. I was making sixteen dollars an hour, plus incentives, which was a generous wage back in 1994. I was also getting overtime pay. My brother worked on a machine called the slitter, and he was making twenty-four dollars an hour. I wanted to stay there and continue working after the summer. I decided not to go back to Georgia and stay in Michigan, but I couldn't stay at the steel plant. They were adamant about the position being only a summer job. I did everything to change their mind, but it didn't work. I had to go.

THE BLUE CRAB

AFTER TWO YEARS OF WORKING OUTSIDE THE RESTAURANT industry, I found myself coming back. I wasn't a huge seafood fan, but when I was a kid, my dad would take my mom to the Blue Crab. I always thought it would be a great place to work. It was a classy restaurant, and the service was always great. The servers even had to wear ties. The Blue Crab had many locations countrywide, and a location on the other side of town wanted to hire me, but I only wanted to work at a specific location. It seemed to be the best of them all.

I applied for the server position and got the job. The two-week training was thorough. I sat down with the kitchen manager first, and she went over all the details of the job, laying out what I would be doing over the next two weeks and who I was going to be working with. Afterward, I sat down with the general manager, Theo. He was a large guy but smooth and articulate. He had an impressive presence, and he was clearly in charge. I knew immediately I wanted to be like him.

The Blue Crab was extremely busy, but it was a well-oiled machine. The staff was always running. Everyone was busy.

They started me out working in the kitchen with a guy named Cameron. Cameron, although a regular employee, ran the kitchen. He was what they called an expo or kitchen coordinator. He made sure all the food looked exactly like the picture on the menu. Once the food was picture perfect and ready, he called out the servers' names and let them know their orders were ready. The server, or someone else, had to get the food from the window. He didn't care who got the food, but that food had better go out. Cameron didn't play.

He started my training by teaching me how to make salads. All I did on my first Friday at work was make salads. I had never made so many salads in my life. And it wouldn't get any better. On Saturday and Sunday, that was all I did. I didn't think people could eat that many salads. I also was a little pissed off because I had applied to be a server, not a salad maker. I did everything for the salads. I stocked the salad bar and kept all the dressings filled. Just when I thought I was doomed to be a salad maker eternally, they ordered me to make soups also. So now, I was making soups *and* salads.

Cameron said since it was slower on the weekdays, I would not only make salads and soups, but I would also start running food to the tables. That freaked me out. I always saw the servers carrying food trays, balancing them on one hand as they took food out to the tables. I was amazed they could carry the food like that without dropping it.

The first time I had to take a tray out to a table, a gorgeous girl named Ciara asked me to follow her. Ciara was not only beautiful, but she was also nice, and she had a body like a Coke bottle. Boy, was she perfect, and she knew it. She wasn't cocky or conceited, but she was aware. She acted like a princess, and I liked her a lot, but I didn't try to talk to her. She was out of my league. Besides, everyone knew Ciara's boyfriend came up there to eat about three times a week, and he always had his boys with him. Word was he had a lot of money. He was also about twenty years older than us. There was no way she would talk to someone like me. But I could look, though!

The tray Ciara wanted me to carry was large. It had three bowls of soup on it and two salads. I said, "I've never carried a tray before."

"Come on, you can do it," she said. "Just carry the tray with both hands until you get used to it."

I followed her like a puppy. I would have done whatever she told me to do. When I went to the dining room with her, she already had a tray stand prepared for me to place my tray. She thanked me and smiled. I melted away.

By my second week of employment at the Blue Crab as a server, all I had done was make salads, soups, and help servers run food to their tables. I was getting pretty good at this thing, but Cameron told me not to get too comfortable because I would soon begin coordinating the food and shadowing a server in the dining room. I was anxious about the idea of shadowing a server. I was getting comfortable working in the kitchen. I didn't even want to serve anymore. Besides, the servers had so much personality. I thought I was too quiet to be one.

WORK RELATIONSHIPS

IDECIDED I WOULD DO A GREAT JOB AS A KITCHEN COORDINATOR, so they wouldn't have to move me out of the kitchen. Although I didn't talk a lot, I could listen. Many interesting stories emerged in the restaurant, and some of them were crazy. Most of the crew hung out together, and several of them were dating each other. Things would get a little messy because quite a few of them were dating or screwing multiple people.

One girl named Miyah was the loudest one of them all. She was dating one of the cooks, Kareem. She laughed about everything. The first time I met Miyah, she came into the kitchen and yelled, "Oh oh, I see we got a new guy!" She introduced herself to me and told me she had been there for two years. She reassured me that if I needed help with anything, she'd be there for me.

Kareem, the cook she was dating, was as 'hood as they came. I don't think he liked her all that much; he was just getting the booty. Miyah was clingy, and she wanted to let everyone know Kareem was her man. She incessantly paged him on his pager during his shift. Kareem's food always came up late because he was checking his pager. I don't know why he didn't turn it off. He constantly denied dating Miyah, claiming she was obsessed with him.

Even though he treated Miyah like crap, it never deterred her. We hated working with Kareem when Miyah wasn't there. He couldn't even concentrate on cooking because of his pager. Every time it beeped, he said, "Aw shit!"

One time, a manager named Stan was working on the line with Kareem, and Kareem kept complaining about Miyah paging him. Stan was getting frustrated with all the beeping as well. Finally, he picked up the pager and told Kareem he was going to put it in the office. When he'd picked it up, Miyah was in the process of paging Kareem. Stan read the message on the pager and saw it was a countdown from ten to one. He dropped the pager and ran off the line. I guess he thought it was going to blow up. We never stopped laughing at Stan for that one.

Kareem treated Miyah poorly, and he never hid that fact. He constantly flirted with other girls in front of her. She'd get upset and cry, but he just shrugged and laughed at her. Some of the girls who worked there told Kareem he was awful for treating her that way. He agreed and often said, in front of Miyah, "Yeah, I know I'm no good, and I ain't shit, so why don't she leave me alone, then?"

It seemed the worse he treated her, the more attached she became. She even let him use her car, which was a big mistake. He disrespected the car the same way he disrespected her. Every time she got into the car after letting him use it, she complained about it being filthy. She'd always find empty beer bottles in her backseat and the overpowering smell of marijuana. He even left the leftover butts from the weed he'd smoked in her ashtray, with a few burn marks in the fabric. Every time Miyah confronted him about the car's condition, he antagonized her and claimed it wasn't him. They both knew it was him, but he would never admit it.

He could do no wrong in her eyes. She was blinded by one-sided love. We thought she finally got it when she ordered our famous Blue Crab melt. The sandwich was one of the most mouthwatering items on the menu, made with lump crab meat and fresh blue crab on top of one-inch Italian bread, with fresh mozzarella, parmesan, and Monterey Jack cheese. It was served warm and toasted to perfection, with cheese and crab meat oozing from every direction. A bib was required to eat the sandwich because it was messy but equally delicious.

The crew ordered the Blue Crab melt often and loved it. Typically, Kareem wasn't our best cook, but when a girl he liked—not Miyah—had ordered it, he made it look amazing, just like the picture on the menu. Everyone was surprised he had put together a great looking meal, inspiring us to order it for ourselves. Miyah agreed it looked great, and she, too, wanted to order one. She placed her order and told Kareem to make sure it looked just like the other one he'd just made.

"Don't worry, I got you. This will be the best-looking crab melt you've ever seen," he promised.

Ten minutes later, Kareem found Miyah and told her the sandwich was ready. Miyah was giddy. She couldn't wait to see the crab melt her man had made for her. But she was devastated when she finally saw it. It was awful, the worst crab melt I'd ever seen. The bread was burnt and he'd added only a pinch of cheese, not nearly enough to ooze.

"Why did you make my sandwich so awful?" Miyah asked with tears in her eyes.

He laughed, brushing her off. Tears stained her uniform as Kareem casually walked away. Miyah was dating Kareem, but Kareem was doing his own thing. A few months later, she became pregnant with his child.

Miyah's sister, Stephanie, worked there also. She was different from Miyah, nice but tough. No one messed with Miyah because of Stephanie. She wore a bandanna to work every day, and she worked in the kitchen. Her boyfriend, Calvin, also worked in the kitchen. He was wild and crazy. Everyone gave Stephanie her space because they knew her boyfriend was certifiably insane.

I'm not sure how he was employable, and I was shocked that Theo had hired him.

Theo made sure everyone adhered to the uniform standard, whether they worked in the kitchen or dining room, but Calvin always looked a hot mess. His hair was all over the place. Some days he came in with an uncombed Afro. The next day, his hair would be in a ponytail. He once came to work sporting Afro puffs. He looked terrible, but no one said anything to him about it. His demeanor dared people to confront him, but we weren't fools. He carried an ax in his truck, and he often took it out when he was in the parking lot, chasing people around with it as a joke. Even though he was playing around, I knew he wouldn't hesitate to use it. He'd probably used it before.

He and Stephanie broke up after he'd gotten mad at her one day. Unlike her sister, Stephanie was as tough as nails, and she didn't take any bullshit. She told us all the story one day in the kitchen after closing.

Calvin began screaming at her, trying to intimidate her. But Stephanie wasn't afraid of him, and she screamed right back. Her response must've surprised him, because he slapped her when she wouldn't back down, hoping she'd shut up. Stephanie slapped him back just as hard. They tussled in the parking lot until Calvin eventually got the upper hand. He picked her up and slammed her onto the ground.

As Stephanie lay there wounded, Calvin walked away. She said she was relieved until she noticed him going to his car and opening the trunk. He went back to Stephanie and bent down in front of her. "You really fucked up!" he whispered.

For the first time, Stephanie realized Calvin was crazy. He smiled as he picked her up and threw her into the trunk. The first thing she saw was the ax, but before she could react, Calvin reached down and grabbed it. He stood there, looking at her, smiling, with one hand on the trunk, the other holding the ax.

She trembled as she feared what was coming next. But instead of hacking her to death, he slammed the trunk close. He kept her in there for hours as he drove, getting in and out of the car at various stops. She could tell he was on the freeway at one point because of the car's speed. He purposely switched lanes and turned quickly, causing her to flop around in the trunk.

Just when she thought the nightmare would never end, the car jolted to a stop. She could hear what sounded like a garage door opening as Calvin drove a little more and finally stopped. He got out of the car again. Although she was relieved the ride was over, a renewed fear emerged as she thought about the ax. Was he going to use it on her?

She began to cry as she imagined her own bloody murder. Then she heard more voices. They were arguing, but she couldn't make out the words. The voices drew closer, and she heard what sounded like flip-flops slapping the ground with each step. She heard fumbling as one of the voices attempted to open the trunk. Stephanie was ready to fight for her life. As she prepared herself for the inevitable, the trunk opened, and she was blinded by the light overhead. As her vision cleared, she realized she was in a garage, and Calvin, his mom, and sister were standing over her.

"Boy, what are you doing with this child in your trunk? Are you out of your mind?" his mom screeched.

"Ma, she disrespected me. You know I don't allow nobody to disrespect me!" Calvin whined.

Calvin's sister burst into laughter. She didn't like Stephanie.

"I will disrespect you if you don't let this girl out of here! Are you trying to go to jail again?"

"Nah, Ma! But if I let her go, she's gonna tell, and I'll go to jail anyway."

Calvin's mom looked down at Stephanie with sympathetic eyes. "Look chile, let this go! My son is a little crazy, but he wasn't going to hurt you. But if you report him," her eyes reduced to slits, "I may let him go ahead and do his thing. You understand?"

Stephanie understood perfectly. She was to keep her mouth shut, and it would all go away. She nodded with vigor. "Understood!"

Calvin offered to drive her back, but she was terrified. His mom jumped into the car and told Stephanie to get in. She was reluctant, but she complied. They drove toward Stephanie's house in silence, except to give and receive directions. When they were a few blocks away from the house, Stephanie lied and told her they'd reached her destination. She didn't want his crazy mom to know where she lived, so she walked the last few blocks home.

She was relieved to have made it through the ordeal, but she was never the same again. She refused to talk to any other guys who were rough and tough—or black.

• • •

No one compared to Calvin, but Cameron was a little strange. He was obsessed with a girl named Nita, but she didn't like him at all, and it was obvious to everyone but him. However, she had no problem using him. She never treated him poorly, but when he wasn't around, she talked badly about him. Cameron did everything for Nita. If she needed a dessert, he made it. If she needed someone to walk her food to her customers' tables, he did it. She played the damsel in distress whenever he was around. When he wasn't at work, she couldn't function because she was used to Cameron doing everything for her. When she tried to get the other guys to do things for her, it didn't work.

Cameron let her use his car anytime she wanted. He often allowed her to drop him off at work and let her keep his car. Sometimes, when he got off work, he'd have to wait for her to pick him up. She was never on time. It was no secret, except to Cameron, that she had a boyfriend. Her boyfriend didn't mind that she was leading him on. He was also using Cameron's car, and Cameron had no idea the guy existed! It was sad to see her using him like that. I was sure her behavior would backfire on her.

Another trainer worked there named Cynthia. She was cool with everyone. She was fun and friendly, always in our faces, talking to us. She never strayed from a conversation. But Cynthia's breath was terrible. She gave new meaning to dragon breath. Her breath smelled so bad, it made my stomach hurt. Everyone kept her at arm's length. She had a boyfriend who worked there as well, but he must've lost his sense of smell and taste prior to dating Cynthia. All his nostril hairs must've been burned off. I couldn't imagine having her in my face all day, let alone kissing her.

One day, I ordered a baked potato, and I had dressed it up perfectly, with butter, sour cream, cheese, and bacon. I seasoned it with salt and pepper. As soon as I took my first bite, Cynthia asked me if she could have a bite. I said, "Sure" and gave her a spoon. It didn't bother me. We weren't going to be sharing the potato.

"This is so good!" she said after taking a bite. Before I could stop her, she dipped the spoon she had eaten from back into my potato.

I was disgusted. There was no way I could eat another bite of that potato. "Hey, you know what, you can have it. I'm not hungry anymore."

"Thanks! You are so nice," she said, beaming.

I looked at Miyah, and she burst into laughter. She later told me I was smart not to eat that potato. I couldn't have agreed more.

SERVER TRAINING

ALTHOUGH I TRIED MY BEST TO REMAIN A KITCHEN WORKER, pleading my case to Theo, I was unsuccessful.

"I hired you as a server, not a kitchen worker. You would be doing a disservice to yourself and our guests. You're very professional, with a great personality, and I don't want you to hide your abilities in the kitchen."

After three weeks in the kitchen, I ventured out to the dining room to shadow a server, which was the second phase of training. They paired me with an experienced server, whom management identified as a trainer. I was to follow her everywhere she went like her clone. She was one of the toughest, militant servers known to man. They called her "Mud." I never knew where that name came from. She had the personality of a drill sergeant, with a short, stubby stature. She even had a buzz cut. She made it her personal mission to torture me.

Mud made sure I knew the proper service sequence of BASED. She drilled me every day. B for beverage first, A for appetizer second, S for soup or salad (but only after the appetizer), E for entrée, and D for dessert. She tested me on the procedure and other information throughout my shift. I was eager to complete training so I wouldn't have to work with her anymore. I didn't see how she made any money as a server. Although she was thorough, she had no personality. She should have been a drill sergeant. She would have done well.

She always fussed at me, telling me all the rules, but one day, she took her militant behavior too far. I was at the salad bar, making salads for her. We weren't supposed to put our trays on the salad bar, and she had reiterated that rule to me on several occasions. For some reason, I wasn't thinking and put my tray down.

Mud came out of nowhere and slapped me on the back of the head. "If you don't take that tray off the salad bar!" she yelled.

I was shocked. I couldn't believe she had put her hands on me. Being hit on the head was my pet peeve. I had a low fade haircut at the time, which meant I didn't have much hair on the back of my head, so when Mud slapped me, it made a loud sound, like someone using a fly swatter to hit a table.

I whipped around and looked her dead in her eyes and reacted from embarrassment. "If you ever put your hands on me again, I will fuck you up!" I warned.

For the first time, Mud didn't seem so tough. My ego deflated as I noticed the fear in her eyes. I felt bad, and I later apologized. I would've never hit her. It wasn't one of my proudest moments. I was embarrassed because I had never spoken to a woman that way. But she'd gotten the point. After the shift ended, she told my managers I was ready to end training, and I was good to go solo. She probably didn't feel comfortable working with me anymore.

I was glad she never told a manager, especially Theo. He was a great guy. He carried himself gracefully and spoke eloquently. He was always dressed nicely, and he was a professional. Everyone knew he ran the restaurant because of the way he carried himself. He always spoke to everyone at the front of the house, and all the guests liked him. In the kitchen, he carried himself the same way, but he was looser. He cracked jokes with the employees, and he was open to letting people crack jokes on him.

He and one of the servers regularly made fun of each other. The server would say something funny about Theo's size, but Theo had the best comebacks, often cracking on the server's teeth. Anytime the server said something about his weight, Theo went on the cook line and grabbed the grill brush. The grill brush was always mangled, although it was replaced every month. It was charred, dirty, and the bristles were in disarray from constantly brushing the grill.

Theo would give the grill brush to the server. "You left your toothbrush at work," he'd tease.

No matter how many times he told the same joke, we laughed.

• • •

I started to like being a server. I wasn't the fastest, but I enjoyed interacting with the guests. One of the guys in my training class was fired after his first shift. The dude looked just like Steve Harvey back in the day. A guest had ordered a strawberry daiquiri and complained that it didn't have any liquor in it. He picked up the drink, took a sip, and said, "Nah, lady, that definitely has some alcohol in it" and set it back down on the table.

When she asked for the manager, he was fired instantly. He didn't understand why he was let go. I had never waited on tables prior to working there, but I knew we couldn't do *that*. Some people lacked common sense.

Serving was fun, and it allowed me to see a different side of people. I didn't realize how much people lied. I waited on a table with two young ladies. One of them ordered a piña colada. Originally, she tried to send it back, stating it didn't taste like it had any liquor. I explained to her that a piña colada was made with coconut flavoring, and it also had coconut rum, so it was hard to taste the liquor because it had the same coconut flavor.

She kept the drink, but when I came back to the table, she said it had a piece of hair in it. *Are you serious?* I said to myself.

She had drunk half the drink and now a dry, long piece of hair was sitting on top. If the hair had been in the drink, it would have been curled up and wet or stuck to the glass. I shook my head. I couldn't believe how many times people did this.

From time to time, I would come to a table, and a mom would be nursing her infant baby. Every mom was different, but I always felt uncomfortable. Some moms were annoyed if I came by while their boobs were out. One lady scowled at me for glancing at her boobs. I didn't do it on purpose. I just happened to walk past and, in my peripheral vision, I saw a titty! I'm a dude. I didn't initially think, *Oh, this lady must have her breast out because she's feeding her infant child.* All I saw was a titty! Once I realized what was going on, I felt uneasy, but it wasn't my fault. She should've covered up or went to the bathroom if she was going to get upset about someone looking at her. It wasn't like I was staring.

Some moms didn't care if I saw them nursing. In fact, they often whipped out their breast at the table while I took their orders. I felt I would go blind if I looked.

I wanted to say, "Hey lady, put it away!"

INDISCRETIONS

P EOPLE OFTEN USED THE RESTAURANT AS A MEETING PLACE for their indiscretions. I saw one of my neighbors at the restaurant regularly. I didn't know him that well, but he lived on my block. His wife was nice and personable. She always spoke to everyone on the block, while he never said anything to anyone. He stayed to himself. He was one of the first people I saw hanging out at the restaurant for a prolonged period. He was always with a woman, who was not his wife. He'd sit at the restaurant for about five hours with the other woman.

He had no idea who I was the first few times he saw me. But one evening, when I was at home sitting on my porch, he recognized me.

He was walking down the street with his wife, and they were holding hands and talking. As they walked past my house, the wife said, "Hello."

I spoke and, initially, as usual, he looked in my direction and didn't say anything. At that moment, he must've realized who I was because he spoke. "What's up, young brother? How you doing?" he said.

"I'm fine. Thanks."

It didn't stop him from coming to the restaurant with that other woman, but he began speaking to me every time he saw me. When he saw me at the Blue Crab, he acted as if we were best friends. I guess he thought we were cool because I never said anything to his wife about what I knew. I never liked him, but it was none of my business what he and his wife were doing. I wasn't friends with either of them. I thought it was a horrible situation for the wife, but it wasn't my problem.

• • •

I once served a table of guests who requested to sit in the back of the restaurant at the very last table. As I took their order, the woman couldn't keep her hands off her date. When I came back to the table, I didn't see her at first, but as I got closer, the guy said something, and she popped up from beneath the table. Now, I could be slow at times, but I quickly realized what was going on. She was giving him a blow job. I laughed about it at first, but when more guests were seated at nearby tables and they didn't stop, I became irritated. The other tables looked around, but she stayed beneath the booth. We had to get a manager, and he kicked them out immediately. Quite a few people got a kick out of making out in public. That wasn't the last time I saw something like that.

I Can't Stop Laughing

ONE EVENING, I SERVED A PARTY OF TWELVE BY MYSELF, A table with eleven women and one guy, who was treating the ladies to everything they wanted. Every one of the sistas at the table was gorgeous. He, however, was a huge, fat, nasty guy. He wore one of those pimp hats with a feather in it. He must've had a lot of money because he repeated, "Money is no object" as I took the orders around the table. I had to let them know about the upgrades they were ordering. Too often, guests ordered something, and after I brought the meal, they'd claim they had no idea about the extra charges. Their defense was their server hadn't told them about the extra cost, even though the charge was plainly visible on the menu. I guess they couldn't read, either.

After he told me money was no object for the third time, I stopped telling them about the upcharges, and I began upselling them on everything. I convinced all the ladies to get the Blue Crabarita (the restaurant's version of a margarita), with an extra shot of tequila. He was drinking Hennessy straight.

At the end of the meal, he wanted to show me that money

didn't matter, so he reached into his pocket and pulled out a thick wad. I didn't know if he was trying to impress me or the ladies. I couldn't care less about him and his money. I wasn't impressed, but I *did* want to make sure he left a huge tip.

We had chairs that rolled, and he was stuffed into his chair like a can of biscuits. When he tried to put the money back into his pocket, the chair shot from under him, going in one direction, while he went the other way. It seemed to happen in slow motion. He was laid out flat on his back.

I couldn't hold in the laughter. I laughed so uncontrollably that I had to run into the kitchen with tears streaming from my eyes. I could hardly breathe. The people in the kitchen were concerned about me because I was crying, but they knew I wasn't distraught when two other servers came running into the kitchen, laughing as well. I still couldn't talk, but one of the other servers explained what happened.

When I finally came back to the table, the guy and his eleven ladies had left. He had given the money to my manager and said he had to go. His bill was well over $500, and he left me no tip. I couldn't blame him after my hilarity at his expense. I guess the joke was on me.

I missed out on a big tip another time as well. I was just about to get off work for the day, and I was to serve one last table. I had no problem taking one more table. It was a woman and a baby, and she said she was still waiting for her husband to get there. After about twenty minutes, her husband still hadn't arrived. My other tables had left, and she was the only one remaining. I asked my manager if I could give the table to someone else, and he said it was okay. One of the other servers didn't mind taking the table, so I introduced him to my table and told the guest I was leaving for the day. I assured her the new server would take good care of her.

As I walked away, I saw a tall guy approaching the table. I made a double take and recognized him as a professional bas-ketball player for the Detroit Pistons. He was the husband the woman was waiting on. I could've kicked myself. The next day, when I came in, the employees were still talking about him. He'd given the server a $100 tip. I had missed out on easy money!

O.J.

FORTUNATELY, THEO WAS OUR GENERAL MANAGER AT A TRYING time for us. He was with us during the O.J. trial. The date was Oct. 3, 1995. Although it was big news at the time, we didn't talk about it too much at work. Predominately black workers were employed at our location, about seventy-five percent black and twenty-five percent white. We all got along well, with no discrimination or favoritism, and I loved it.

I was at work when the verdict for the O.J. trial came down. I was in the kitchen, and we had all turned the radio on. Several customers had their portable radios on in the dining room as well. When the jury was about to announce the verdict, the restaurant was silent with anticipation.

"We, the jury, find the defendant, Orenthal James Simpson, not guilty."

The restaurant exploded with mixed emotions. All the black employees and guests cheered. We jumped up and down, hugging each other, while a lot of the white employees and guests were visibly upset. No one tried to hide their emotions on either side and, for the first time, I saw division amongst us. Just three years prior, the nation had witnessed Rodney King being beaten nearly to death, and all those horrible police officers had gotten away with it. So many of us were celebrating the fact that the justice system had finally ruled in our favor.

Despite our differences, Theo did a masterful job of keeping us together as a unit. When he noticed the verdict caused a divide, he immediately gathered everyone into small groups and set the tone.

"Although there are mixed reactions regarding the verdict, we are to remain professional," he advised. "You are all allowed to express your feelings, but once we break from the conversation, leave it alone. And I don't want us talking to the customers about the verdict, either."

Over the next few shifts, he connected with each employee to ensure the conversation about the trial was left outside. The O.J. verdict didn't have a lasting effect on us, however. After about a week, the conversation started to die down, and we went back to normal.

Everyone loved Theo, but he wasn't there too much longer. He transferred to a different location. I noticed that managers didn't usually stay at the same location for long. Typically, the general manager stayed longer but not the lower ranking managers. Theo had already been there for some time, so it was time to switch things up. We all missed him.

They replaced Theo with Tim, and he was nothing like Theo. He wasn't personable or caring, and he acted as if he hated being there, from the time he stepped foot into the restaurant. Theo was like a brand ambassador for the company. He used to be out in the dining room kissing babies, shaking hands, and opening the door for the customers and employees. He added a home-like feeling to the place. Tim rarely came out of the office. If he did leave the office or the kitchen, it was only to walk out the front door. Often, he had the other managers let him out the back door. He barely knew our names and never gave an effort to learn them.

The only time he went to a table was if another manager wasn't there or a customer demanded to speak to the general manager. When that happened, he didn't even know the table number. He had to get someone to show him where the table was. The only other time he visited tables was if our area director called and stated that he was coming by. Then he went into action.

LADIES, LADIES, AND MORE LADIES

ONE THING I LOVED ABOUT WORKING AT THE BLUE CRAB WAS the ladies. There were about five women to every guy. I was in heaven. I liked most of the women. I never tried talking to Ciara, but it didn't stop me from liking her. Another woman was about ten years older than me, and she was even sexier than Ciara. She was married, with two kids, and her name was Kandace. She was out of my league, but I was infatuated.

A set of twins worked there as well. They were both cute, but one of them was a straight up freak. It all started when she gave me a hug. The hug lingered and turned into groping. She would squeeze by me whenever we were in a tight spot, and she'd always find a way to brush her butt or her body against me. If she found me sitting at a booth, she slid in beside me and fondled my man parts underneath the table. She also did it if we were at the end of the bar, waiting on drinks from the bartender. I never minded one bit. I looked forward to working with her. But she was a tease.

She let me drop her off at home sometimes, and we would sit in her driveway, kissing and fondling each other. After she got me aroused, she'd say she had to go. I'd ask to come in or invite her to my place, but she never would. I got tired of the game, but I continued to let her touch me.

I liked another girl, too. She was a hostess, Danielle Hawk. She was my type: short, red bone, and sexy. She had a mole on her face, right next to her nose, but it was seductive. We never did talk, but she frequently caught me glancing at her and vice versa. We always gave each other a slight smile, but that was it.

One day, I finally had the nerve to talk to her. We were having an all-restaurant meeting. We were used to seeing each other in our uniforms, but we weren't required to wear uniforms to the meeting, so we dressed up to show everyone how we looked outside of our work clothes. I was no different. I put on my new kicks and a new outfit. I thought I was fresh to death like a million bucks. I had just gotten my new car the day before, a four-door Toyota Camry with a sunroof and shiny rims. I thought I was the man, coming up to the job in my new car. I had my shades on as I bumped music from the speakers.

As I exited the car, I saw Danielle walking up to the restaurant. Because of my shades, she couldn't tell I was checking her out, but I could see that she was checking *me* out. I took off my shades and gave her the Detroit head nod (a quick upward nod that most young Detroiters give for acknowledgment). I was feeling myself and trying to be cool.

Once the meeting started, I sat far from her, on the other side of the room. I knew she was feeling me, and I was feeling her, but I still had to be smooth. We glanced at each other from time to time, but neither of us made a move. After the meeting, I finally said hi to her. She was with the same friend she was always with. Her friend seemed mean, but I never paid her any attention.

As we talked, I found out she was only sixteen. I had immediate visions of having to go to prom, and there was no way. As cute as she was, I knew she was too young for me. I didn't want any parts of that. I was a twenty-year-old grown man.

From time to time, I went out with some of the girls I worked with, but it never went anywhere. I went out with one young lady named Constance. She was a little loud and liked to be seen and heard. I thought she was cute, so we hung out at a bar one night. We were having a good time until she said she had to go to the bathroom. The bar had large booths that allowed plenty of privacy. We couldn't see over the booths while sitting down.

Constance was gone for a while, so I got up to check on her. When I stood up, I saw her at the bar, getting a phone number from another guy. I was furious, but I was too nice to go off on her. I wish I would've left her at the bar. When she came back to the booth, I mentioned I had seen her at the bar. She brushed it off and said it was some guy she knew. I knew she was lying. I also knew there wasn't a chance in hell for a second date.

I was interested in another girl named Kendra, who worked in the kitchen. She was a little on the 'hood side. One time, when we were leaving, she had one of the bartenders sneak and make her an alcoholic drink and put it in a takeout cup. She asked me to take it out of the building for her. "You should take it. They won't say anything to you or think you would sneak out a drink."

I agreed to take it, of course. However, as I was walking out, someone bumped into me, causing me to spill the drink. It was a strawberry daiquiri, and the smell of rum was pungent. As soon as the drink spilled, she turned and went the other way. I couldn't believe she was going to let me take the fall. I could've kicked myself for being so gullible. I knew I would never talk to her again.

TAMEKA

I WENT OUT WITH OTHER GIRLS WHO WORKED THERE, NOTHING serious, but that changed when Tameka walked in the door. She was a new server. I had become a pro at serving, and the managers had me training the newbies, so they paired Tameka with me. She wasn't a red bone, but she was fine and sexy. She reminded me of Nia Long, one of my movie star crushes.

I found myself being a little nervous around her. To overcompensate for my interest, I was a jerk. I was hard on her during her training. I could tell she was the type of girl who always got attention. All the guys at the job were already trying to holla at her, so I gave her no attention at all, just like James had taught me. She probably got the best and most detailed training ever. I loved being in her presence, but I never let on to it. I critiqued her harshly and told her she had to complete her menu training and know the menu 100 percent before she even thought about following me on the floor. I gave her assignments to complete and checked them thoroughly on her following shift. I checked everything, even her uniform, like a drill sergeant.

As the next few weeks went by, she was trained and ready

to be on her own, and I was relieved. But it was bittersweet. I couldn't wait to get away from her and be myself, but I also hated that I wasn't going to be with her. I'd see her, but I rarely spoke to her. I saw how the other male employees and customers salivated over her, and I continued to keep my distance. But she always came to me and asked questions. I answered her sternly and kept it moving.

One evening, Tameka was off work, which meant I could concentrate on my guests without playing a one-sided game to ignore her. Everything was going well, and I was making good tips. I was at the end of the bar, waiting on the bartender to prepare my drinks and, out of nowhere, Tameka came walking in. She was off work and coming by to get food. This was the first time I'd seen her without her work uniform. She already stopped traffic with her uniform on, but in regular clothes, she was breathtaking. She wore Guess blue jean shorts that fit her just right, with a white, tight-fitting shirt, with the Guess logo across her chest. She normally wore her hair in a ponytail at work, but that day, she wore her hair loose and flowing.

Her legs were perfect. As a matter of fact, everything was perfect. She was killing it. I started to get dizzy.

"Hi, Carter," she said as she passed me.

"Hi," I managed. Before I knew what I was doing, I made the mistake of saying, "You look very nice today." I couldn't have just said she looked nice, but I had to add "very." I couldn't believe I had let that slip. And it didn't go unnoticed.

As if in slow motion, Tameka turned around. "No way! I actually got a compliment from *you*?" Her smile covered her face.

I tried to play it cool, but I couldn't stop smiling, either. I was relieved I had finally said something nice to her.

She came over, put her hand on my head, and jokingly said, "You must have a fever, or you're not feeling well." She laughed. "Thank you." She gave me a long, tight hug.

Checkmate! She had me. I was done. Toast. It was over. I melted.

From that moment on, we talked every day at work. She always came near me and bumped into me. Every time she came to work, the first thing she did was give me a hug. We'd play all day at work. I loved coming to work and hated when I'd come in and find out she was off for the day.

Things started to go up another notch as we began to get closer. We were trying to act like best friends, but it was more than that, and we both knew it. Tameka didn't have a car and always had to get a ride home from her dad. I told her it would be no problem for me to take her home on the nights we worked together. At first, she told me I didn't have to do it, but after a while, she said she'd love it if I dropped her off.

The first time I dropped her off, we sat in front of her house, talking for hours. I hated to leave, but she said she had to go. She had a daughter, and she needed to put her to bed.

As I prepared to leave, I tried to play it cool, but she called me out.

"Stop trying to be so tough. I don't want you to go, and you don't want to leave, either. Now, give me my hug!" She leaned in to embrace me, but we ended up kissing, and it seemed to last an hour. When we were done, she looked and me, smiled, and whispered in my ear, "I really like you."

It was over. She was going to get all of me!

Things blossomed between us quickly after that first kiss. I became her chauffeur. She wasn't trying to use me; I offered. I was young and single, with no responsibilities, so it didn't bother me to help her out. I enjoyed being with her every second. She had a young kid, and she lived with her dad. I was still living at my dad's place, so we didn't get a lot of alone time, except when we were at work or I was driving her where she needed to go.

She spent the night with me once, and we had a great time. My dad thought she was cool as well. She left a note on our refrigerator in the morning: "Goodbye, Dad. Have a great day!" I got a kick out of that. She was a special girl. I was already twenty, and this was the first young lady I really liked and wanted to bring around my parents. I had dated young ladies before, and we spent time together, but I had never wanted anyone to meet my parents. Tameka was the first girl I introduced to them as my girlfriend.

My oldest brother sighed with relief when I told him about her. "Bro," he said, "it's about time. I was beginning to wonder!"

"Wonder what?" I asked.

"I don't know. You never brought any girls around. A brotha was starting to wonder if you liked them."

We laughed, and I assured him that wasn't the issue. I held my family sacred and was never interested in bringing just any old chick around.

My dad thought things were serious between Tameka and me when I asked him to help me fix up my old car. It was my first car, a 1984 two-toned brown and tan Chevy Monte Carlo with T-tops. I loved the car, but I was putting too much money into it, and it kept breaking down on me. After spending money on a new engine, it broke down again, and I was done with it. That was when I got my new Toyota Camry. Once Tameka and I were together, though, I decided to fix the car up so she could have it.

My dad and I worked on it until it was drivable. One of my boys drove up to the Blue Crab in the Monte Carlo and parked it for me. Tameka was at work, and she had called me to pick her up. Much to her surprise, when I picked her up, I was standing outside. She gave me a strange look because I would usually wait for her in the car.

"Where's the car?" she asked.

I gave her the keys. "I want you to drive."

She shrugged and took the keys, but she didn't see the car because I had parked the Camry on the other side of the building. "What's going on?"

"Follow me," I said. "I have something to show you." We walked toward the Monte Carlo. "We're driving this car today."

"Whose car is this?"

"It's yours."

She put her hands over her face and almost cried. "I can't take it. I can't believe you bought me a car!"

"I didn't buy it. It was my old car, and I fixed it up. Get in and drive it home. I'll see you tomorrow."

It felt good to do that for her. I wanted nothing from her except her love, and she expected nothing but the same from me. I was the talk of the town when I went back to work. The girls were in awe. But Tameka didn't like the fact that everyone knew her business and people thought she was using me. Several days after I had given her the car, she brought it back to me and said she simply couldn't accept it. I pleaded with her to keep it, but she wouldn't. As much as it hurt me for her to give the car back, I respected her for the decision. We were too early into the relationship for me to be doing things like that.

We continued dating and having fun for the next few weeks, but things started to change. As I got to know her, she started telling me more things about her. She had been with her daughter's father for almost four years before they'd broken up, and her baby was three years old at the time. They dated in high school and had the baby right after she graduated. She and the father had just broken up not even two months before she started working at the Blue Crab. So, although our relationship was new, she never had time to get over her past lengthy relationship. Her daughter's father was still involved in her daughter's life. We never crossed paths, but he and Tameka still talked daily because they had history together and a child.

As the saying goes, things that happen too fast end just as fast. Tameka and I went from being in a new, exciting relationship to not hardly speaking. She said I was a great guy, but everything was happening too fast, and she needed space. I couldn't fathom the thought of giving her space. I couldn't leave her alone. I constantly called her and pleaded for her to spend more time with me. It got so bad that she ended up quitting the Blue Crab. Too many people were in our business and questioning her about why she had dumped me. They assumed she had dumped me after I had given her the car. They didn't know she had given it back several days later.

She got a job at a restaurant down the street. I came in as a customer, so I could sit in her section and tip her. Boy, was I desperate for her, but it pushed her away even more. She finally told me I had to stop calling her and stopping by, that she would contact me when she was ready to talk. I knew she meant business, and I didn't want to push her away any further, so I granted her wishes, hoping she'd change her mind.

Weeks went by, and I never heard from her. I would park at the end of her street, so I could see her when she came out of the house. I only did it twice because it was too much for me to see her when I couldn't touch or talk to her, and she would've had a fit if she'd seen me. I told myself I had to let her go. Sadly, I did, but I thought about her often.

That was my first big heartbreak.

Man Up!

I couldn't shake my split from Tameka, and I was depressed at work. My coworkers tried to get me to go out with them and have fun. I would go, but I never had fun. I was faking the funk. The break up took its toll on me at work. My performance started to decline. One of my managers, to whom I didn't talk that much, made it clear. She told me to man up! She was as rough as any man I knew, but we called her BT behind her back, for "Big Titties." She was a big woman with huge boobs but acted like a dude. She wasn't gay, just 'hood. I often wondered how she got the job as a manager.

She told me to come over to the smoking section. That's usually where we would find BT. We could work an entire shift without seeing her unless we needed something because she was always sitting down in the smoking section. Quite a few of the veteran servers would often be in that room, talking to her daily. Even some of the kitchen crew would sit down with her.

I always noticed the crew going in and out of the smoking section when BT worked, but I never paid it too much attention. I didn't care for her. She was too 'hood and unprofessional. The more she talked to them, the less she talked to me, so when she asked me to come into the smoking section, I was surprised. I knew I hadn't done anything wrong.

"Have a seat at one of the booths toward the back," she said. "I'll be right back."

A few seconds later, two other servers came over and sat down with me. They were two of her so-called buddies. I asked them what was going on.

They laughed and said, "Just be cool."

We talked for a few minutes, and BT came back with drinks on a tray: a Long Island and three shots. She set the Long Island in front of me. "What kind of drink is this?" she asked.

I thought she was testing me on the drink menu. I knew my alcohol sales hadn't been up, but I didn't think this was necessary. I still had tables to get back to. "I know what it is; it's a Long Island."

"I'm glad you know what it is. Now, drink it."

"What?"

"You heard me. Drink it!"

I thought it was a setup. If I got caught drinking, I'd be terminated.

As if she knew what I was thinking, she said, "Don't worry about getting fired. You can't get fired if the manager is the one to give you the drink."

She and the other two servers slammed their shots. They all slapped the shot glasses back on the table and looked at me.

Convinced, I started drinking the Long Island. After taking a few sips, I said, "I have to go check on my tables."

"Don't worry about the tables. I have someone else watching over your tables already," BT explained.

"But I don't want the rest of my drink."

"Drink it, now! It's time you put some hair on your chest and stop walking around here in a stupor because of that girl! So what she dumped you. Get over it! There are too many bitches out here to be worried about one. Now, drink the rest of it."

They all left me at the table alone with my thoughts. When I was just about done with the drink, BT brought me a shot and told me to wash the drink down with it. After I drank the shot, she said, "Now, get back to your tables, and I don't want to hear you talking about that bitch anymore. You got it?"

"Yep."

I was buzzing badly. I wasn't thinking about my tables, but it didn't seem like BT was offering an alternative, so I went back to serving. For the first time, I dropped a tray of water on the floor as I walked out of the kitchen. Some of the servers, who knew I had been drinking, laughed at me. All I could do was laugh as well. For the rest of the night, I had fun at work for the first time since Tameka had broken up with me. I made great money that night as well.

For a while, I thought BT had my best interest at heart. She offered me drinks at least once a week. I became one of the people going over to the smoking section to hang out. But I learned that was how BT got people to do anything she wanted. She never did any work. She just sat in the smoking area, and she never had a bad shift because she fed drinks to the people working for her. I later found out she did this with almost everyone. She'd feel them out first to see if they were cool, and she'd make them drink to hold it over their heads. She knew no one would ever tell on her because it would be their word against hers, so she was always able to get away with doing nothing. I still didn't care for her, but I did care to get the free drinks and food from time to time.

Time's Up!

I STAYED AT THE BLUE CRAB IN MICHIGAN FOR ANOTHER MONTH, but I was looking for a change of scenery. I had been thinking about moving out of state prior to dating Tameka, but when I met her, I put all my plans on hold. When the relationship ended, I decided to make the move. I had been talking to my brother, who lived in Georgia. I had gone to college there and always liked it, so I decided to move there. I had no money saved up or a place to stay, but I did it anyway. The plan was to stay with my brother for a couple of months, while I saved money to get a place of my own.

I told management about my decision, and they told me a transfer would be no problem. I'd just have to find out which location I wanted to go to and contact the general manager to make sure they had an opening for me. I knew there was a Blue Crab a couple of miles from where my brother lived. I got in contact with the general manager, and she said they were looking for more servers. I was elated and put in my notice.

On my last day at the Blue Crab in Michigan, we were slammed, and everyone was making a lot of money. I was grateful for the busyness because I needed every dime to move. I was hustling but moving too fast, and I made a grave mistake.

Servers carry a check presenter when taking guests' orders. It holds the pads we use to jot the orders down, but most servers also leave their tips and coupons inside the pockets. Mud told me to *never* leave money in my check presenter, and, most importantly, we were to never set it down anywhere! But halfway through my shift, I set my check presenter down on the salad bar so I could remember all the different salads I had to make. Once I'd made the drinks and salads, I put them on the tray and started walking out of the kitchen. I must've gone five feet when I realized I had left my check presenter on the salad bar. I immediately stopped, turned around, and dashed back to the kitchen. My check presenter was gone. I had been gone for maybe twenty seconds. I started panicking and asking everyone if they had seen it. Everything was in that check presenter, all my money and the restaurant's money.

I knew the rule was to never leave money inside the check presenter, but I thought I was responsible enough not to lose it. There was almost four hundred dollars in there. I couldn't afford to lose that money, let alone pay the Blue Crab back. I was devasted and pissed off. I knew someone had stolen it. But there were about fifteen people in the kitchen, and there was no telling who the culprit was.

I panicked. "Who has my money?! I know somebody took it!" I shouted.

The other servers asked me where I'd put it.

"It was on the salad bar."

A few servers started helping me look for it. We looked everywhere, on the floor, behind the salad bar, on the cook line, and in the dish area, but we couldn't find it.

Someone finally looked inside the trash and found it. She held it up and asked, "Is this yours?"

For a moment, I was relieved. It was, indeed, mine. My coupons and credit card slips were there, but all the money was gone. I was breathless and devasted. Not on my last day at work! I didn't want anyone to think I had conveniently "lost" the money on my last day. It just didn't look good.

As I surveyed the kitchen, fuming, I noticed everyone had helped look for the money except for one dude named Leon. He was standing there with a smirk on his face. I couldn't stand him, and he didn't like me either. He tried talking to Tameka while I was dating her, and he'd tried even harder when we broke up. She wanted nothing to do with him, and that bothered him. He never spoke to me, but when I was in a slump about the breakup, he always came over to say hello with a smile. I was pretty sure he was the one who had taken my money.

I walked up to him. "You need to run me my money," I said.

He turned to me quickly. "I know you not talking to me."

He was, undoubtedly, waiting for an opportunity to fight me, and I had so much built up anger that I was ready to knuckle up as well. Just as we both started toward each other, someone walked between us and someone else began rubbing my back and pulling me backward. It was Miyah. She told me it wasn't worth it to lose my job and my opportunity to transfer. I knew she was right, so I walked out of the kitchen.

I had forgotten I had a table waiting on their salads and drinks. As I walked past them, they grimaced at me. I quickly regrouped and walked back into the kitchen to get my tray. I'd returned to the kitchen so quickly that everyone thought I was coming back to fight Leon. They all got excited, including Leon, but I just grabbed my tray and walked out. I wanted to slam the tray of food on his head, but I kept walking.

After I checked on my tables, one of the managers asked me to come to the manager's office. When I got there, Leon was there with another manager. They wanted to know what happened.

"I was in the kitchen, minding my own business, when Carter walked up to me, ready to fight," Leon explained. "When he became confrontational, I remained calm and tried to converse with him about what was going on."

That was some B.S., and he knew it.

"Why don't you tell us your side, Carter," the manager said.

"I *did* come at Leon," I admitted, "but not to fight, to confront him for stealing my money."

"Did you see Leon take the money?" the manager asked.

"No, I didn't."

"Did anyone else see Leon take the money?"

"No."

They chastised me in front of Leon and instructed me not to say anything else to him, and if I had a problem with another employee, I was to come to them. I assured them I understood, while Leon sat there with a sly grin.

As we were about to leave the office, the managers told me to stay and asked me what happened to my money. I told them the story.

"How do you plan to return the money to the Blue Crab?"

"I'll figure it out, even if I have to borrow it."

"It is unfortunate that you lost the money, but you have to turn it in by the end of the day."

Once again, I assured them I would figure it out, and I left the office.

I started thinking about how I was going to make up the money. It was almost four hundred dollars in cash payments, plus sixty dollars in tips. There was no way I could make that type of money back in tips by the end of the day.

Although I hated to do it, I decided to ask my mother to borrow the money. The original plan was for me to work that day and hit the road to Georgia early Saturday morning. I would have one day to chill out and go to work at the Georgia Blue Crab on Monday. But now, I would have to work for the rest of the day and Saturday just to pay my mom back. I would essentially be working for free for the next two shifts.

I returned to the dining room and started taking tables again. I wasn't doing a good job because I was only thinking about the money, not giving great service. I wanted to turn and burn the tables: get in, get tips, and get out. I was able to accomplish two of the three. I got my tables in and out, but they weren't tipping me well because my service sucked.

I had already worked for about five hours, and since I was planning to work that night, I asked my managers if I could take a small break to eat. They granted me the break, and I sat down in the backroom by myself. I ordered a kiddie burger because that was all I could afford.

As I sat there sulking, Miyah and Ciara came to talk to me. They both believed shady Leon had stolen the money, but there was no way to prove it. I started getting angry again.

Ciara soothed me. "Miyah got with all the servers, and they collected some money, so you can pay back the Blue Crab," she said.

"Everyone knows you're a great guy, and you didn't steal that money. We're family, and everyone likes you," Miyah added.

They had collected $350 from the other servers. I was in disbelief and touched that everyone had done that for me. I paid the money back to the Blue crab, and I was forever grateful to Ciara, Miyah, and the rest of the employees. I was relieved that I didn't have to borrow from my mom or work on Saturday. I promised Miyah and Ciara I would stay in contact with them, and I gave them both big hugs before leaving.

When I got home, I packed up my Camry and went to sleep early. It was time to hit the road first thing in the morning. As I fell asleep, I replayed Miyah's gracious act in my mind. I was grateful.

MOVING DOWN SOUTH

THE TRANSFER TO THE GEORGIA BLUE CRAB WENT SMOOTHLY. I was settled in by Monday. The new location was much different from the one in the North. Everyone was slow, but the guests didn't seem to mind. Even they had a laid back demeanor.

During my time up North, I had never experienced a guest get upset with me or curse at me. Things were different in the South, however. On my first night working there, I had an issue with a table. I was taking the customer's order, and he didn't know what he wanted. I told him I could give him a few minutes if he liked.

He said, "Yeah, why don't you do that," and he waved me off to dismiss me.

I thought, *Where they do that at?* But I was cool. I said, "I'll give you all the time you need."

I went ahead and took my other table's order, and when I was on my way to the kitchen, the guy tried to stop me and tell me he was ready to order. I waved him off and dismissed him, just as he had done me. I knew I was terribly wrong, and I don't know why I did it, but it felt good to do it. A few minutes later, I found myself in the office with my service manager and the general manager. The general manager's name was Elma, and she was like a police officer. She was even tougher than BT. Elma was Madea before Tyler Perry created the character. She tore me a new asshole.

"I'm thinking about firing you right now!" she growled. "I don't know how they do it in Michigan, but they don't play that mess here in Georgia! You came highly recommended, but I can't believe you did something like that. If you are *ever* rude to a guest like that again, you may as well walk right out the door, because I will not hesitate to fire you. Do you understand?"

"I absolutely understand," I responded with my head down.

I knew she wasn't playing around. I had to get my act together immediately. I didn't move all the way to Georgia to get fired.

A sheriff came every night and sat in the lobby, unbeknownst to me, because of the neighborhood. The guests were terrible, but most nights, we didn't need the security, especially when Elma was there. Her presence was like having a police officer in the building. Not only did she keep us in line, but she also didn't play with the guests. If the guests were rude or tried to play like they had no money to pay the bill, all we had to do was send Elma to the table. She took no prisoners, ordering customers to leave her building immediately.

One thing I liked about working for Elma was the unlimited amount of hours available to work. I worked for tips, so the more I worked, the more I got paid. I never concerned myself with the check. Most servers don't. We made $2.13 an hour, and we were taxed on our hourly rate plus our tips. If we worked forty hours per week, our check was only slightly above eighty dollars before taxes.

I didn't look at my check until after a few months. I knew I had worked every day for the past week, and on at least three of those shifts, I had worked a double. I had worked at least sixty hours that week, which was normal for every week since I'd gotten there. But when I looked at my check, it stated forty hours worked. I examined some of my past check stubs when I knew I had worked about sixty hours, and they all said forty hours worked.

I brought my check stubs to Elma to talk about it. She was straight up with me.

"I'll allow you to work as much as you want and make as much in tips as you can, but I'm not paying any overtime," she said.

"But that's not fair," I said. "If I worked sixty hours, I should be paid for sixty hours."

She broke down the money for me. "I don't allow overtime pay, but if you were to get overtime, you would still only be getting approximately $3.20 per hour. Do you make more than that per hour in tips?"

"Yes."

"Then do the math. If you're making at least twenty dollars per hour in tips, with an extra twenty hours per week, I am allowing you to make an extra four hundred dollars in cash tips a week. I'm not going to pay overtime, so I can schedule you for only forty hours per week and cap you off right there, but understand that I will not let you get one minute of overtime. Or, you can make an extra four hundred a week in tips. Which option do you want?"

The decision was clear. "I'll take the extra four hundred."

I spoke to a few other servers, and they told me the same thing. They didn't mind working the extra hours because they were getting paid. I didn't realize it was illegal. She was getting free labor out of us.

Elma stayed for about a year while I was there before they sent her to another location. She was known for fixing up the restaurants, and she was doing it, albeit illegally. Unfortunately, anyone who came behind her and did the right thing would be at a disadvantage. They couldn't run the same type of labor hours Elma ran because she was willing to cut corners. I realized the southern locations didn't maintain the same moral standards as some of the others. Hence the term "The Dirty South."

THE DIRTY SOUTH

WHEN I FIRST STARTED WORKING THERE, I DIDN'T TALK MUCH. I kept to myself and minded my own business. A dude named Anthony worked there. Everyone called him Ant, and he looked just like an ant. He was skinny, with a big head and huge Coke bottle glasses. He looked like someone from the old *Fat Albert* cartoons. Ant was my opposite. He never would shut up, and he stayed in everyone's business. He was irritating. I usually walked the other way when I saw him coming. It was a good thing I worked mostly day shifts, and Ant worked the night shift. When he was coming in, I was leaving.

One day, I decided to work a night shift. What a huge mistake! I ended up working a section with Ant, and he never stopped talking! He talked not only to me but everyone working. He'd even be in the back, talking to the kitchen people. It didn't take me long to realize why he was talking to everyone. He was the restaurant drug dealer. He had never offered me anything, but that was because we never talked.

We were standing in the dish area, breaking down our dirty plates, and I heard him ask someone if they needed anything. I knew he was talking about drugs. They told him they were good, meaning they didn't need anything.

As he walked away, I asked him, "Do you know about my other job?"

He was startled at first because this was the first time I had said something to him. He finally said, "Nah, what's your other job?"

I reached into my back pocket and took my wallet out. I flipped it open and flashed it quickly like the police, showing a badge. "I work for the police department," I said with a firm demeanor.

I tried to keep my face together, but Ant looked like he was about to run out of the building. I laughed as I told him I was just kidding. I had to tell him. I had never seen a grown man pee on himself, but Ant looked like he was about to do just that. I had to tell him again that I was just kidding because he didn't move.

Once he realized I was joking, he was overjoyed. He told me he was, indeed, about to run out of the building. Now, I was about to pee on myself because I was laughing so hard.

After we had both calmed down, he asked me if I needed anything. I shook my head. I knew he was going to end up in jail.

Ant thought my joke was so funny that he told everyone what happened. Although most people thought it was funny, two guys didn't. They were both dishwashers and apparently good friends. They always worked at night together, playing around and giving the servers a hard time. And the servers were often frustrated because the dishes were usually backed up because the guys were horse playing. Every time someone said something to them, they were defensive and argued.

Tony was the more aggressive one. The other guy, Rob, did more talking and laughing, but he was the most irritating one. Rob usually got the argument started, but Tony took it to another level, cursing and carrying on.

Neither Tony nor Rob cared for me much, and the feeling was mutual. It all stemmed from when I had left some dishes in the bus room and told them I would be right back. When I came back to break the dishes down, Tony cursed at me.

"Don't ever leave this shit over here no more!" he barked.

I was dumbfounded. Just when I was about to say something back to him, my manager, Barbara, walked up. She'd apparently seen what happened and motioned for him to go with her. A few minutes later, I saw him with his bag, and he was leaving. He gave me a smirk before he left.

Barbara had sent him home for the day and wrote him up. Rob was pissed off because he had to stay and do the rest of the dishes by himself.

From that day on, the two of them had an issue with me. Every time they saw me, they called me a teacher's pet, but I ignored them. One day, Tony bumped into me. When I approached him, he looked as if he was ready to fight. I was ready as well. Once again, a manager was around and stopped us before anything happened.

"What is going on?" she asked.

"Carter was being aggressive," Tony said.

I shook my head. "No, he just shoulder bumped me on purpose!"

He acted like an angel, claiming it was a simple mistake. Both my manager and I knew he was full of shit, but no one was around to vouch for what happened.

These dudes always had something to say to me, but I continued to ignore them. Every time I came near them, Rob attempted to instigate an argument between Tony and me. "Yo, Tony, this guy keeps staring at you like he wants to do something!" he'd say.

"He don't want none of this!" Tony responded while staring at me.

I continued to disregard them. They were idiots, and I wasn't about to get caught up in their foolishness.

Tony and Rob were two of Ant's best clientele. They didn't like the fact that I was messing with their dealer. When they found out I had tricked Ant into believing I was a police officer, they started in on me again. I didn't want to lose my job, but I wasn't going to get punked, either. I didn't know how much more I could take. But just before things got worse between us, Tony was fired for getting into an altercation with one of the cooks.

The cook was an older guy who seemed volatile, just like Tony. The dish guys constantly made fun of him and always had something smart to say. One day, the cook was in a horrible mood and decided he wasn't going to take any lip from anyone. When the two guys started bothering him, he went to the dish area and confronted them.

"Get out of my face, old man, before I fuck you up!" Tony warned.

The cook picked up one of the kitchen knives and pointed it at them.

Rob stepped back in fear. "Man, you're crazy. We were just playing around with you," he whimpered.

The cook smiled at them. "You two don't seem so tough, do you? I don't hear you talking now!"

"Just like I told you before, get out of my face, old man, before I fuck you up!" Tony repeated.

The cook didn't move as he maintained a menacing smile. Rob was frozen, in fear for his life. Tony, however, stood his ground, smiling back.

"What you standing there smiling for, young buck?" the cooked asked.

"For the last time, I'm telling you to get out of my face before I fuck you up, *old man*."

"I should stick this knife up your ass and teach you a lesson, *young buck*." He stepped toward Tony, but before he could take a second step, Tony reached into the backside of his jeans and withdrew a gun, pointing it inches from the old man's face.

Although he was crazy and volatile, the old guy wasn't prepared for the threat. He knew he had messed up. He'd brought a knife to a gun fight, literally. His expression changed immediately. "Look, man," he whined, "I'm sorry. I was just playing. I wasn't going to hurt nobody." He looked as if he was about to faint.

Luckily, someone had alerted Elma about the situation. She walked right up to them like she wasn't afraid at all. She looked at Tony and commanded, "You put that gun down right now, young man!"

With the gun still pointed at the old man, Tony looked at Elma with a threatening leer. Everyone was afraid that Tony was going to shoot the old man. The cook seemed convinced as well.

With more authority in her tone, Elma yelled, "Put that gun down, and get out of here!" She had no fear but, for the first time, she showed compassion. "Tony, it's not worth it. You're going to spend the rest of your life in prison if you pull that trigger. Now, once again, please put that gun down and walk out of here."

He thought about it and slowly lowered his gun. As he walked away, he looked at Elma and said, "I guess I don't work here anymore." His smile remained as if it were tattooed on his face. Just before he left the kitchen, he put his gun away.

Everyone was shocked, even Rob. He didn't know his friend was that crazy. It all happened within two minutes, but it seemed like twenty. I was in disbelief. I had been close to getting into an altercation with that guy, and who knows what could've happened.

After Tony left the building, the police came quickly, but Tony was long gone. They took a statement from Elma and arrested the old line cook. He was stunned that he was being arrested after having a gun pulled on him. He'd forgotten he'd instigated the situation by first pulling a knife. They talked to Elma and wrote a report. They also requested information about Tony.

Once the police left, Elma told everyone to get back to work as if none of it had phased her. She was a beast!

We never knew what happened to Tony. As far as we knew, the police never caught up with him.

Sonny Days are Here

Shortly after the gun incident, Elma was transferred to another location, and part of me wondered if she demanded the transfer. They replaced her with another general manager named Sonny. He was the opposite of Elma. He was professional and knew how to talk to people. He had a high focus on training and developing people the right way. Sonny seemed to enjoy his job, and he was passionate.

After all the drama and dealing with Elma, I had begun to sour on the idea of working there. However, with Sonny steering the ship, I was beginning to enjoy working for the Blue Crab again. I had asserted myself as a skilled server, and quite a few guests would ask for only me. Because of my stellar reputation, I started training people again. Sonny and I talked all the time. He liked the way I carried myself and told me I should think about going into management. I hadn't thought about it before, but I was fairly interested.

Although Sonny was professional, Rita, one of his kitchen managers, was not. She was only a few years older than me. She was shapely and always wore tight pants that showcased her butt.

She drove the guys crazy with her behind. I, however, couldn't stand her. She was unprofessional and didn't know how to talk to people. I couldn't have cared less about her nice behind. I always walked the other way when I saw her coming. Most of the time, we didn't have to worry about her approaching us unexpectedly because she spoke loudly. As soon as I heard her voice, I went in the other direction. I doubt if she knew or even cared.

She had to grab a towel and wipe off a handprint from her backside almost daily. The guys in the kitchen were required to wear powdered gloves that left residue on their hands. They frequently grabbed or rubbed her behind, leaving the residue on her pants. She'd play dumb and act like she didn't know where the handprints came from, but it got old when it began to happen almost every day. How were we supposed to respect her as a manager if she carried herself that way?

One Friday night, we were swamped. I had a table that had been waiting a long time for an order of fried cheese squares. It had been fifteen minutes already. The fried cheese squares typically only took five minutes to prepare. When I went into the kitchen to check on them, Rita was on the cook line, working the fry station. I asked her how long it would be before the squares were ready.

"It'll be ready when it's ready!" she said.

"It's already been fifteen minutes, and the guests are asking for them."

"It'll be ready when it's ready," she repeated.

Frustrated, I walked away. When I went back to the table, the guests were upset because their appetizer still wasn't ready. I had already brought the salads to the table because they needed to eat something. I went back to the kitchen and saw that my table's entrées were almost ready, but they still didn't have their appetizer.

I was polite when I asked Rita again if the squares were ready.

She whipped around. "If you can't wait for them, come and cook them your damn self."

I was usually respectful and compliant, but I had a problem when people got loud and confrontational with me. I walked around to the cook line and proceeded to cook the cheese squares. I hadn't cooked anything at the Blue Crab before, but I knew they couldn't be hard to make. They were already cooked, just frozen. I had seen the cooks take six squares out of the bag and put them into the fryer.

When I walked onto the line, Rita yelled, "Get off the damn line!"

I ignored her and proceeded to cook my squares.

She said it even louder. "Get off the damn line!"

I continued to cook. It only took about two minutes before they were ready.

She walked off the line and onto the expo side, standing there with her arms folded. I could hear her telling servers she was going to get me fucked up for that. It didn't bother me one bit, because I wasn't concerned about her or anyone else. Once I got my cheese squares ready, I walked off the line and took them out to my guests.

As I walked past Rita, she said, "Oh, you think you are *so* fuckin' funny!"

I ignored her, even though I wanted to go off on her.

When I was done waiting on my tables, she approached me. "I'm sending you home for being insubordinate. You can talk to Sonny about it if you still have a job tomorrow."

I didn't mind going home because I didn't want to say anything else to her, but I didn't want to lose my job.

I didn't know, while she was planning to send me home, the other manager on duty, Barbara, was getting on her for how she carried herself. She told Rita she wouldn't allow her to send me home. She and Rita got into it, but Barbara must've won because I didn't go home. For the rest of the night, Rita was fuming. I stayed away, although I laughed at her and her immaturity, unaware of my own.

The next morning, I was scheduled to work, but I knew I

had to see Sonny before I started. I was a little nervous about how things would go. Once I walked in, I immediately went to the manager's office to discover my fate. To my surprise, Sonny wasn't in the office, but the office door was open. The managers wrote inside a green book every shift, and the book was sitting on the manager's desk. Video cameras were located throughout the restaurant, and the main camera station was in the office. I looked at the monitor and saw that Sonny was in the kitchen. I quickly looked at the green book to see what Rita had added. She had written a novel about me. It was one-sided and made her look like a saint. She stated that I had yelled at her and pushed her to the side. I couldn't believe it! Everything she said was a lie. I was heated, but I had to regain my composure. I went straight to Sonny and asked if we could talk.

The moment Sonny saw me, I could tell he was irritated. I kept my cool. Once we sat down and began to talk, he expressed how disappointed he was in me, but before he made any decisions, he allowed me to tell my side of the story.

As I began to tell my side, Sonny started turning red. He kept stopping me and asking me if I was telling the truth. I assured him I was being truthful. He looked defeated and distraught about having a manager who had acted in that manner.

I admitted I was wrong for walking on the line and making my own food. "I was completely out of line, and that shouldn't have happened, but at no time did I ever disrespect her by yelling at her or cursing at her," I explained.

"Did you ever push her?" he asked.

"I did not."

"Write down everything you've said in detail. You have to go home. You're suspended until I get more information."

I was nervous about getting suspended. For the second time since I had been in Georgia, I found myself in trouble. I couldn't explain to my brother that I had been fired. I lived with him and his wife rent free, but I was planning to move out, so he and his family could have their home back. I didn't want to be a liability for them.

My suspension only lasted three hours. After getting my statement, along with statements from other people who were working at the time of the incident, Sonny realized I was telling the truth. He called me and asked if I wanted to work that night, and I told him I was on my way.

Once I got to work, Sonny apologized for what had occurred. I found out later that Rita had gotten written up for her inappropriate behavior, and I was happy about that. She was mad at me for a few months and barely talked to me, but I couldn't care less.

• • •

I was working an evening shift one night when Rita and Sonny came walking through the kitchen with a tall, attractive woman. It took me a moment to realize it, but I knew her. We looked at each other at the same time, and she screamed, "Carter!"

"Veronica!" I yelled.

Veronica was one of my managers at the Blue Crab in Michigan.

"What are you doing here?" I asked.

"I'm moving to Georgia, and I'm transferring to this location."

She looked at Sonny and asked, "Now, how is Carter? He better be good! I groomed him myself."

"Carter is one of my best," Sonny boasted.

Rita rolled her eyes, with her arms crossed. "So, you two know each other?" she asked.

Veronica said, "Yes, he was one of my favorite servers back at home."

Rita looked like she was about to vomit. Sonny interrupted and said he wanted to get back to giving Veronica a tour of the restaurant. Veronica and I hugged, and she promised she would see me soon. She wouldn't be starting for another month. I couldn't wait for her to come on board.

SLAVE AUCTION

I LATER FOUND OUT THE BLUE CRAB WHERE VERONICA AND I had worked in Michigan closed a few months after I had left, and Veronica was unhappy about how the company handled it. The Michigan location was in a rough area. There had been a shooting there between guests, and someone was shot in the leg. With all the constant issues and threats, the store was losing money, so corporate decided to close the location. When looking back, everyone could see the writing on the wall, but it was still a surprise to them all.

I called my old friend Miyah, and she said the entire crew was pissed. The way the closing was handled reminded her of a slave auction. They were instructed to attend an all-restaurant meeting, which was no surprise because we often had those meetings two to three times a year. But this meeting was different. Multiple general managers were there from different Blue Crab locations in the metro area. The director of operations was there as well. Tim, the general manager that everyone hated, announced, effective immediately, the restaurant was closing. He'd said it as if he had no care in the world. Sensing that and hoping to avoid an all-out riot, the director immediately took over. He stated that the restaurant wasn't making any money. It was losing money, and with all the potential threats and dangers, it was in the company's best interest to close it down.

The employees were disgruntled and started shouting at the director. He was cool and calmed everyone down. He had some of the general managers from visiting locations come up to the front with him. He introduced the managers to the team and ensured everyone that if they chose to stay with the company, they could be transferred to one of the locations run by those managers.

Half the room walked out, cursing. The other half stayed, and that's when the auction started. The remaining employees separated into three groups, and they all took turns talking to the general managers, trying to sell themselves on being picked. Everyone thought the process was horrible, and they should've been given a warning. But the company, however, was afraid to give notice because they feared massive employee theft the day before closing. I knew some of the people who worked there, and I knew it would've happened.

The managers and the general manager were all safe. They were immediately transferred, with no threat of losing their jobs. Veronica transferred to another location as well, but she was done with the Blue Crab in Michigan.

VERONICA RULES

VERONICA WAS AN AWESOME MANAGER. I ATTRIBUTE HER FOR making me a stronger server. Back in Michigan, when I had first started serving, I was slow and needy. We would run a skeleton crew for lunch because it wasn't as busy as dinner. However, the lunch servers had to be on top of their game. We had to be fast and self-sufficient. Often, for lunch, we had no busboys or expo. We could handle bussing our own tables, but not having an expo to coordinate our food and make sure it went out hot was difficult. The bartender wasn't available half the time because he would have tables as well. So, if we worked lunch, we had to hustle.

Veronica was one of the managers who did it all. She cooked, bartended, took tables, and washed dishes, and she never even got dirty. She was one of the best-dressed women I had seen. She wasn't only a pretty lady, but her work ethic was through the roof.

When I came to her, crying because it was hard for me to keep up during the lunch shift, she wasn't listening much. I complained that it was too much, trying to dress our own food and make drinks, while still waiting on tables.

Veronica said, "No problem. We will just put you on two tables for the next month until you can catch up."

Everyone knew that if Veronica said, "No problem," it meant she was done with the situation, and I picked up on that immediately. I quickly told her I didn't want to go down to two tables; I just needed help.

"You simply need to be faster," she retorted. "If you're looking for help, it isn't going to come. If you want to make the money, you have to go get it. You're running fewer tables than anyone else in the restaurant, but you need the most help."

I took the hint. I was pissed at her, but I knew I didn't want my days or tables reduced. I had to hustle. From that point on, I decided if I was going to stay, I had to be faster. Veronica sat down with me from time to time and gave me pointers, but she told me she wasn't about to hold my hand. I knew, by her actions, she meant it.

I saw how Veronica handled people, and I loved it. She never got upset or angry. She did have a way of cocking her eyebrow like The Rock when she was irritated, but that was the only way we could tell she was bothered. She always maintained her composure. She never fired anyone unless they disrespected her, but no one ever did that. She had a mantra that I later adopted: "You can either do it or not do it; it doesn't matter to me. Either way, the job is going to get done." She meant it was our choice whether we were going to do the work. She wasn't going to make us do anything. But we were to choose wisely because if we chose not to do it, we would find ourselves unemployed. Veronica was quick to make the decision for someone who didn't want to work. She would jump in and do it. The work she did was always better than anyone else's anyway.

She also never had to deal with attendance issues for long. Veronica was fair and showed compassion, but if the employees were lazy or liars, she had no tolerance for it. If someone had constant attendance issues, she never called them to see if they were running late. Once they came in, she'd nonchalantly say,

"Oh, I thought you weren't coming, so I had your shift covered." People would be upset about it, but she would shrug. "Oh, well. I didn't think you were coming, but go ahead and enjoy the rest of your day off."

If their tardiness continued, she usually had someone else cover their next three or four shifts. One employee had explained that he was having car problems and said it wasn't fair. She responded, "Well, take the next three to four days, and get your car in order. We will see you after that." He was pissed, but it wouldn't take people long to realize Veronica wasn't playing. She expected us to be at work at our scheduled times. She used the same tactic with people who didn't call or show up for work. She'd tell them, "I thought you had quit, so I gave up the rest of your shifts for this week and next week." She never had an issue with them again.

I was excited about Veronica coming to Georgia. With her and Sonny together, the restaurant was going to be great! I later found out that Veronica was replacing Barbara. That was probably why Rita was so happy when she saw Veronica coming in.

Once Veronica came to the restaurant, she made an immediate impact. I had already told people they needed to get their act together because she didn't play. She became the kitchen manager, and Rita became the bar and host manager. I don't think Rita liked the change because she wasn't a people person; however, she was a horrible kitchen manager. Our kitchen was run by a lot of long-term kitchen workers, who were good at what they did but had strong personalities. Although Rita ran her mouth a lot, she didn't know what she was doing. She was all talk. The kitchen people ran over her, so they weren't too happy when they saw Veronica come in. They tried to run their game on her, but it didn't take them long to see that she was nothing like Rita.

I'd heard she'd gotten into a little trouble with our employee relations department for giving people weeks off for improper behavior and attendance issues, so she started documenting tardiness, and after the third time, she fired the employee. She'd fired about four people in less than three weeks after she'd gotten to our Georgia location. The word was out, and our aggressive kitchen crew knew not to mess around with her.

Walking Out

WE HAD ANOTHER MANAGER NAMED ROBERT, AND HE WAS trying to become a general manager. He was a serious guy and, for the most part, did everything the right way. He was a little standoffish and didn't talk to me much, but I didn't care until I noticed he also didn't listen. I had become a strong server. I could turn tables well. I was fast and focused on getting guests in and out. The managers loved me for it, and Robert was no exception. Every time I worked with Robert, he put me in the smoking area. The wait was always shorter. Although I made good money working in the smoking section, I disliked it because I would go home smelling like an ashtray. I never noticed it until I got into my car at the end of my shift; however, the money always made up for it.

As I handled more tables, I noticed Robert would increasingly give me more. I asked Robert not to put me in the smoking section. Although I was making good money, my level of service was declining. I couldn't handle having eight to ten tables at a time. No one could handle that many tables and give excellent service. My fellow servers didn't want to help me, either. They complained that I was making a lot of money, but I couldn't even walk my own food to the customers' tables. I couldn't keep up. No one would run my food. It would sit under the heating lamps, drying out until I could get to it. I asked Robert every day to put me back in the main dining room, and every day, he said, "Okay," but I still ended up in the smoking area.

One day, he let me work in the main dining room, and it was a piece of cake. I didn't have too many tables, and I could take care of my guests. However, since I wasn't in the smoking section, he put two servers there in my place. I couldn't believe it! He'd always put me there by myself.

I asked Robert, "So, why did you put two people in the smoking section today, but when I work it, I'm always by myself?"

"I didn't think one person could handle it," he replied.

"Exactly! Neither can I."

He chuckled and told me I could handle it.

That irritated me. The two servers who worked the smoking area told me working the section wasn't that bad. "There's two of you, that's why!" I yelled.

They thought I was just complaining. They couldn't comprehend that I was doing the work of two servers combined.

The next day, I came to work and, once again, I was working in the smoking section and, once again, I was by myself. I asked Robert to give me some help, but, as usual, he said I could handle it. I told myself to get over it and do the best I could, but that lasted for only about an hour. I had five tables going. I was taking an order at the fifth table when the hostess seated another. I gave her a look. She shrugged and came back with another table. Geez! I wasn't even done taking the order at the previous table, and now I had two more. I knew the food had to be ready for two of the other tables, and one guest was waiting to give me her credit card for payment. I was "in the weeds." That's restaurant lingo for when a restaurant worker is overwhelmed and can't keep up with serving their customers. I was *deep* in the weeds! I surveyed my tables, and the guests looked disgusted. I was embarrassed and ashamed for delivering that kind of service. It wasn't my fault, but I still felt horrible. I couldn't take it anymore.

I took all the money that was owed to the Blue Crab out of my pouch and put it in an envelope. I went up to the hostess, who had shrugged at me, and handed her the envelope. I told her to give it to Robert.

She said, "Who is going to take these tables?"

I shrugged and walked out of the building. I had quit.

As I walked out and got into my car, I felt refreshed. But five minutes later, I started to panic. I had quit! Reality started to seep in. What was I going to do? I was no longer living with my brother rent free. I had an apartment and a car note. How the hell was I going to pay my bills? I was terrified. I wanted to go back to the Blue Crab and say, "Psych, I was just kidding!" But I knew that wouldn't work.

There is no way I'm just going to go home, I said to myself. I had to find a job immediately. I went to several places and applied for positions. As I made my rounds to fill out applications, I passed the Blue Crab again. Right across from the Blue Crab was a steak house. I went in and applied. They were slow at the time, so the manager decided to give me an interview on the spot. I nailed the interview because I had to. I was desperate! They offered me the job right then. They told me they were having an orientation the next day, and I had to be there.

I said, "Absolutely!"

I was relieved. Almost three hours after I had walked out on my job, I landed a new job.

I got back into my car and, instead of going home, I stopped by a Mexican restaurant to get double fisted. I ordered a Texas margarita and a beer. I needed the buzz. After that, I went home and slept like a baby.

The next day, I went into orientation, early and ready. Everyone seemed nice. The general manager came by and introduced herself. She said how excited she was to have us onboard. The trainer came by and gave us some drinks. She told us the training would last almost two weeks. I was an experienced server and ready to hit the ground running. I had forgotten about the training process. I knew I had to master their menu and operations, but I couldn't afford to be in a training class for two weeks. I decided I was going to be the most attentive trainee they had. I would take their menu home and study it all night if I had to. My bills weren't going to wait.

Although the restaurant was open and had guests coming in and out, my attention didn't wander. I had no time to daydream. My bills were sitting on my shoulders with their arms crossed, looking at me. So, when someone shouted my name, I didn't flinch. I didn't know anyone at the restaurant, so they must have been calling another Carter. When the person shouted my name again, I knew they were saying *my* name, and I knew that voice. It was Rita.

She said, "What are you doing over here?"

"I'm training and working over here now."

"Get your butt back across the street. You don't belong here."

I thought she would've been relieved I wasn't at the Blue Crab any longer. Maybe she had let our past go. She probably realized *she* was the problem.

"What are *you* doing here?" I asked.

"I came over here to borrow some takeout boxes. I thought that was you sitting over there. You need to come back home. I will talk to Sonny," she stated.

"I'm sorry, I work over here now."

"Boy, bye!" she said with a dismissive wave. "I'll see you tomorrow!" She walked out.

On the inside, I was happy. I didn't want to leave the Blue Crab, but I wanted better treatment. From that point, I had zoned out of orientation. I tried to pay attention, but my mind was no longer on working at the new restaurant. I wanted to go talk to Sonny and hopefully get my job back.

Welcome Back

THE NEXT DAY COULDN'T COME FAST ENOUGH. WHEN MORNING finally arrived, I got to the restaurant just as they were opening. The first person I saw was Veronica. She said, "Hello," but her eyebrow was raised. I knew she was disappointed in me.

"I'm here to see Sonny," I said.

"Okay. How is the new job?"

"It's okay, but I was hoping to still work here."

She shook her head and went to get Sonny.

Sonny and I sat down, and he expressed his disappointment in how I'd handled the situation. He gave me the opportunity to speak, and I voiced my concerns about how I didn't think it was fair for me to take so many tables. "I don't like giving crappy service, and I had expressed my concerns to Robert multiple times, but he never gave me the help I needed."

Sonny agreed that no one should have that many tables, but he reiterated how disappointed he was in me for walking out. "You could've come to me, but walking out is unacceptable."

Humbled, I pleaded my case. "I understand, and I respect your decision to terminate me if you must. But if you allow me to stay, you will never have a problem with me again."

To my surprise, he agreed to bring me back but said I must apologize to the management team.

"No problem!"

As I walked out, I saw Veronica again. I told her Sonny had allowed me to come back, and I apologized for letting her down.

I could tell she was still disappointed and not in agreement with Sonny's decision. "You should be very happy I'm not the general manager because I absolutely wouldn't have let you come back."

I was upset that I had disappointed her. I vowed to do whatever it took to get back on her good side.

The next day, I came back to work, and Robert was there. I approached him and apologized for my behavior.

He said a curt, "Okay."

He was pissed that I was still employed. He had nothing else to say to me. I understood. I wouldn't have let me come back either, but I was grateful for the second chance. Robert added me to the floor plan, and I was no longer in the smoking section. He put me in the smallest section, with the least number of tables. I knew this was a punishment, but I decided to give exceptional service to every guest I received. I planned to get back into his good graces.

I overheard some of the other servers talking amongst themselves: "That's some bullshit. They brought Carter back after he walked out!"

I couldn't have agreed with them more myself. I put my head down, kept my mouth shut, and went to work. That was probably why Sonny had agreed to bring me back. I never caused any ruckus. I was always a hard worker and quiet. I would only get upset if there was something stopping me from giving great service to my customers.

I was out to show everyone that Sonny had not made a mistake by bringing me back to work. I especially wanted to show Sonny he hadn't made a mistake. I wanted to do whatever he needed from then on. It didn't matter how many tables they gave me or how large of a party, I would shut my mouth and work with no complaints. And I kept my promise until Sonny bailed me out again.

MLK DAY

It was Martin Luther King Day, and we were busy. I was waiting on a large party of twenty people by myself. Everything went smoothly. The food came out fast, no one had to wait on drinks, and I was having a great time with the customers—until it was time to pay. They wanted to pay separately. I hated when a large party wanted separate bills. It took too long to process. They also had an issue with gratuity being added to their bills. I could see how it was going to turn out.

After I separated the checks and passed them out, the customers wanted me to combine some of the checks. Again, this was no problem, but as I attempted to do it, they said I was taking too long and wanted the gratuity removed. I had waited on these people for almost two hours with no issues, and they didn't want to leave a tip! It was ridiculous. Some of them started getting impatient and began standing up. At that point, I didn't want their tips. I couldn't believe they were behaving like that. I did everything to keep my cool, even when they started yelling at me.

The bartender was nearby, so I politely asked her to get a manager. One of the ladies heard me and yelled, "Go ahead and get 'em."

I practiced patience as I continued processing payments and trying to ignore them, but I overheard another guest say, "I can't believe it's MLK Day, and our own people treating us like this!"

Another customer with them shouted, "Nah, he ain't one of us. He a white boy!"

I was furious. There was nothing I hated more than being called a white boy by another black person because I was professional and spoke properly. Well, the professional part was about to go out the window. Luckily, Sonny approached before things got out of hand. The customers had circled me. Some of the ladies grew louder as they complained to Sonny.

"Our server sucked!" one woman spat.

"I could take it if he sucked, but he was also rude!" said another.

I maintained my composure as I continued passing out the split checks while listening as they all lied to Sonny about how rude and nasty I was. Sonny did his best to try to calm them down, but they were all talking at once.

"He gave us the wrong check!" someone else yelled.

"We've got to get back to work. This is taking way too long!"

"The food wasn't even good!"

Sonny promised he would get to everyone, but he could only help one person at a time. They were growing more impatient, even with Sonny helping them. I was glad he could see, first-hand, their terrible behavior. As he talked to them, I continued passing out their checks. I was ready to be done with them.

While Sonny had his back to me, talking to one of the ladies, I processed the payment for another. She pointed at my face, about an inch from my nose. "It's sellouts like you that make it hard for other black people," she said.

I was getting irate, but I remained calm and simply backed away from her. As I stepped back, I accidentally stepped on one of the ladies' feet behind me.

"Aw, hell no! He just stomped on my foot!" she screeched.

Her outburst got the rest of the people in the party excited again.

"Ma'am, I did *not* stomp your foot," I said. "I accidentally stepped on your foot after your friend pointed her finger in my face."

"Nah, you did it on purpose!"

I shrugged and looked at Sonny. He seemed just as confused as I was. He looked helpless like he didn't know how to handle it.

"You need to fire this rude so-called server!" the woman said.

One of the men at the table stepped up. "Forget getting fired. He about to get it now!"

I was done keeping my composure. They were threatening me. I didn't care how many people there were; I was ready. I threw the remaining bills on the table. Sonny knew I was ready to lose my mind because he put his hand on my chest and pushed me backward. Because of all the commotion, several other workers came over to see what was going on. Two of them grabbed me and walked me away.

"Yeah, muthafucka, walk away!" I heard as I left.

We went into the kitchen. Robert was in there, and he told me to chill and hang out back there. After Sonny diffused the situation, he came to check on me. "Are you okay?" he asked.

"Yeah, I'm okay. I'm sorry for losing my composure, but they were threatening me," I explained.

"You can go home for the day."

I thought I was fired. But the next day, when I came to work, Sonny didn't mention the situation.

Let's Get 'Em

Once again, I was grateful for Sonny and how he'd had my back. And I had Sonny's back as well. One day, we were just opening, and a single guy came in to eat. About twenty minutes later, another server told Sonny the guy had come in there before.

"He's going to eat and sneak out without paying," she warned.

As she spoke to us, the guy got up and went to the restroom. Since I didn't have a table yet, Sonny grabbed me, and we stood in the lobby. A few minutes later, the guy came out of the bathroom and started heading toward the door.

Sonny walked toward him with the bill in his hand. "Excuse me, sir. You haven't paid your bill."

The customer walked backward toward the door. "I left the money on the table," he said nervously.

"Young man, there is no money on the table. You need to take care of this bill."

The guy turned around and ran out the door.

Sonny and I looked at each other simultaneously. Before I could say anything, Sonny said, "Let's get him!"

Without thinking, we started running down the street, chasing him. I had on an apron, and so did Sonny, because he had been in the kitchen, prepping food items. I was catching up to the guy, but he split off the main road and ran behind a row of buildings. I had a flashback of myself chasing that scamming customer at the ice cream parlor years prior. That guy had a knife, and there was no telling what this guy would have on him. I remembered the desperation I felt, standing in the alley with a knife pointed at me. I didn't want to get stabbed or shot. I thought about how stupid we looked, chasing a customer down the street, and I gave up the chase.

Sonny caught up with me and asked, "Where did he go? You almost had him!"

I told him he'd run behind some buildings. Sonny didn't want to venture behind the buildings, either. As we were about to walk back to the restaurant, a cop car pulled up and asked us what was going on. They had seen us both running down the street. Sonny explained to the cops what had just happened. They told us to jump into the backseat and show them in which direction the guy ran. We jumped in and pointed behind the row of buildings. We didn't see the guy anywhere. The police went down another road and behind more buildings. We spotted the guy sitting down against the back of a building, panting because he was out of breath.

We shouted, "That's the guy!"

The cop pulled up on him quickly and jumped out of the car. The guy was too out of breath to even move. The cop handcuffed him, and a few seconds later, two other police cars pulled up. They put the guy in the back of one of the police cars and drove us back to the restaurant.

Sonny was excited and told everyone what happened. I couldn't help but think about how stupid we both were. I was happy, however, that I was able to be there for Sonny for a change.

Don't Mix Business with Pleasure

Sonny and I became almost like good buddies after the chasing incident. Sonny did everything by the book and was a good manager, but I could tell when he started liking one of our bartenders, Michelle. That was a problem. Not only was he the general manager, but he was also married with children. Michelle and I were cool. She was a white girl, but she liked black guys. I think she liked me, but the feeling wasn't mutual.

We often went for drinks down the street with other coworkers when we got off work. Sonny frequently asked me about her. He wanted to know where we hung out. He was trying to feel me out to see if she and I were fooling around. Once it was apparent we were just friends, he started flirting with her. He'd let her eat anything she wanted without paying for it. He was more of a kitchen type of guy, but we started seeing him hanging out at the bar when she was there.

Any time we worked at night together, Sonny asked me to go have a drink with him after work, but he would ask Michelle as well. He told her I was going too, figuring if I was going, she would also go. She always went if I asked her, but he had it wrong. He thought she was going because of me, but she knew he had a thing for her and would buy her whatever she wanted, so she didn't mind going. I went out with them a few times, but it didn't take me long to realize I was the third wheel. I couldn't hang with them when it came to drinking, anyway. Sonny would buy us fishbowl-sized margaritas, and I could never finish mine, but he and Michelle always finished theirs and ordered more. I didn't know my limit, but when I felt like I had to throw up, I knew I had to tap out.

I was so drunk when leaving the bar one night that Sonny and Michelle had to follow me home to make sure I made it safely. They should've just taken me home or gotten me a cab. I woke up that morning, still in my car at my apartment. I didn't remember how I'd gotten there or how long I had been asleep, which was a problem. I could've gotten into an accident and killed myself or someone else. I knew my days hanging out as the third wheel were over. No more!

I don't know what happened with Sonny and Michelle after that, and it was none of my business. I still saw Sonny hanging out at the bar when Michelle was at work. I don't think Michelle was interested; however, she didn't seem to mind the attention or the free drinks and food.

Sonny didn't stay at our location much longer. He eventually transferred to a newly opened location. About a year later, I heard he was fired because he was fooling around with one of the workers there. The server he was messing with had threatened to tell Sonny's wife about them unless he gave her some money. He took money from the back safe at the restaurant to pay her. One of the other managers, who didn't like Sonny, knew about the situation and contacted the area director. The area director popped up at the restaurant the next morning. He let Sonny do all his counts, including the money, and when Sonny didn't seem alarmed about the missing money from the safe, the director asked him to recount the money in front of him. Sonny wasn't prepared. He had no explanation for why the money was short. He was suspended, but after they investigated more, they fired him. I don't know if Sonny's wife ever found out why he wasn't working any longer. I'm sure he made up something. I hated to hear that about Sonny, but he was bound to get into trouble. Managers were prohibited from messing around with workers—and stealing money.

New Leadership (Again)

Veronica was promoted to general manager when Sonny transferred to a different location. Everyone was worried because Veronica didn't play around. Although Sonny was a good GM, everyone knew Veronica would be top notch. The first thing she did was get Rita out of there. She didn't fire her, but she was on Rita so much every day that Rita ended up quitting.

Robert had to watch out as well. Prior to Veronica's promotion, she and Robert got along. But it seemed Robert resented Veronica for getting the promotion before him. He tried to give her a hard time, but Veronica wasn't having it. She sat down with him quickly and set the stage, letting him know she was in charge. She also knew he was a good manager and promised him, if they worked together, she would help him get to the next level. That won Robert over quickly and he jumped on the Veronica train.

Veronica was a great GM. She took away all the nonsense. She took no prisoners. She was professional and fair, but it was not a democracy. It was Veronica's way, or we'd be seeking new employment. We all quickly understood that she followed all the standards of the Blue Crab, and if we didn't follow the standards, we had no argument.

She made us more professional but more fun as well. She made sure every birthday or celebration our guests had was enjoyable. If they chose the Blue Crab as their meeting place for a celebration, we were to go crazy and give the ultimate service. She made sure we sang to every table, and she put me in charge of creating birthday songs. She wanted us to have many different songs that were lively and entertaining. Sometimes, on a Friday or Saturday night, there could be five or six birthday celebrations going on at the same time. Veronica didn't want us being redundant, going around to each table sounding like robots. Our songs became so fun that we never had a problem getting other team members to join in. Even the kitchen folks would come out to sing sometimes. One of my favorites was when I would put my sunglasses on and act like I was Stevie Wonder, singing his "Happy Birthday" rendition. My customers always enjoyed that one. It was always a lively event and, often, the other customers in the dining room joined in. Those were good times!

Veronica was instrumental in making me look at my future with the company. I had never thought about going into management. I still wasn't thinking about it, but she was in my ear. Veronica gave me knowledge about the 401K plan and getting insurance. I hadn't thought of those things on my own. I was out there free living, not thinking about my future.

I Think I Broke My Leg

Rita was replaced by another manager named Sean. He was cool, but he made it clear he was only there short term. He wanted to get restaurant work under his belt, but his trajectory was to work at the corporate office. He had to spend a minimum of six months in operations to get in at the corporate level. Sean was by the book. He was professional when dealing with both the guests and the crew. We knew he would make it to the corporate level and be successful.

I had no issues with Sean until I had to call off work one day. Because I stayed only three miles from the restaurant, I never left home for work until ten minutes before my shift started. Because I had stayed up late the night before, I didn't wake up on time. I was supposed to be at work at eleven a.m., but I had gone to sleep at around five that morning. So, when my alarm went off at ten, I kept hitting snooze.

The last time I hit snooze was at 10:43. That meant I had exactly seventeen minutes to shower, put my clothes on, and get to work. I jumped out of bed, but there was one problem: My leg had fallen asleep. I lost my balance and fell. While trying to catch myself, I hit my head on the desk in my room and severely hurt my knee. I had cut my head on the fall, and it was bleeding, but my leg was throbbing. I was in so much pain! I thought I had broken my leg or knee.

I gathered my breath, but I didn't call anyone for help, not even 9-1-1. While I was still sprawled out on the floor, I called the Blue Crab. I was in grave pain and holding back tears as I dialed. Sean picked up the phone. At first, he didn't know who I was because I was wailing in agony. I was finally able to tell him I was lying on the floor, and I thought I had broken my leg.

"Let me guess, you're not going to make it to work today?" he said sarcastically.

I shouted, "Sean, I think I *broke my leg!*"

"Well, make sure you bring in a doctor's note before you return to work!" He hung up the phone with no empathy.

I knew he probably encountered a lot of call-offs, but to act as if he didn't care was unacceptable in my book. I was furious, but I was in too much pain to worry about it. Still on the floor, I called my mother in Michigan. She was a nurse and would know exactly what to do.

She was alarmed when I called. "Honey, are you okay?"

"I think I just broke my leg getting out of bed."

"Can you move your leg at all?"

"I haven't tried." My leg was still folded beneath me in an awkward position.

"Try to move it a little."

Although it hurt like hell, I was able to unfold my leg.

"If you can move it, it's not broken," she explained. "Run some hot bath water and put some Epsom Salt in the tub."

I told her I would call her back when I was done. I slowly dragged myself into the bathroom. I had to pull myself up and run the water. Once the bathtub was full, I climbed in and lay in the water. It was scalding, but with the Epsom Salt, it was working. I stayed in the tub for over an hour. I didn't want to move. I kept adding hot water, but after an hour, the running water wouldn't stay hot any longer.

I was finally able to get out of the tub. However, I couldn't put any pressure on my leg. After managing to get myself dressed, I drove to the emergency room. They said I had severely sprained my knee and leg. They put an air cast on my leg, gave me crutches, and told me to stay off my leg for two weeks. I made an appointment to come back the following week. After they gave me some pills for pain, I left and immediately drove to the Blue Crab with my doctor's note. I was planning on giving Sean a piece of my mind.

When I entered the restaurant, he was in the lobby. As soon as he saw me with the crutches, he looked sick. "Oh, Carter! I am so sorry for not believing you," he said. "I'm just so tired of all the call-offs, and I've heard so many B.S. stories that I'm just numb to it. I feel horrible! If you can stick around, I will buy you lunch."

I accepted his apology, and I was glad he apologized because I was about to go off on him. This time, there would've been no Sonny to protect me. I know Veronica would've fired me for that nonsense.

GIRLFRIEND

Although I was out there free living, I managed to have a girlfriend. She was a hostess at the restaurant, and she was a little younger. Her name was Ebony. She used to play around with me and flirt, but I thought she was too young. I asked her how old she was, and she told me she was about to turn twenty. That wasn't bad; I was only twenty-two. She was cute, but I had never thought about dating her. We didn't have a first date or talk on the phone. I'd just go over her house and hang out. She lived at home with her parents, and she was the only child. When I stopped by, we talked in her driveway because her parents were usually home. We never kissed or hugged; we just talked.

One day, she asked me to come over, and I said, "Sure!" I thought we were just going to talk again. When I got to her house, her parents' cars weren't there. I still didn't think too much about it. Although I was attracted to her, we had never even kissed before. I had no idea that was about to change.

As soon as I walked into her house, she walked me upstairs to her room. I had never seen any part of her house except the family room and kitchen. I was caught off guard. I didn't even have a condom. Well, she had thought about it all. She already had a condom waiting for me.

As she undressed in front of me, she said, "Come here." Suddenly, she didn't seem so young anymore.

We started hanging out every day. I wasn't prepared for someone like her. She wanted to have sex every day, several times a day! I was cool with that, but she wanted to have sex everywhere, and she would always set me up. She didn't work as much as I did, so anytime I was at work and she wasn't, she called the restaurant and told me she had brought me something to eat. I never wanted food from the Blue Crab because I ate that stuff all the time, so when Ebony brought me something else, I loved it. When I could manage to get a break and come outside, she'd be sitting in her car, and I'd get in and give her a kiss.

"What do you have for me?" I'd ask.

"Me!"

The next thing I knew, she was trying to unzip my pants. I tried to stop her, reminding her that we were in the parking lot at work, but she didn't care.

"Be on the lookout," she instructed as she put her head in my lap.

I decided to be the damn lookout, and I found myself being the lookout on several occasions in the parking lot.

One time, I didn't do such a good job being the lookout. As I concentrated on her, some of my coworkers came out of the building and started walking toward the car. I saw them just in time and was able to alert Ebony to stop. She lifted her head, and I suspect my coworkers knew what was going on because they kept walking past the car. Ebony laughed, and I panicked. If it had been Veronica walking outside, we both would've been fired. She didn't care, but I needed my job. I told her I couldn't be the lookout anymore.

It wasn't until I had a girlfriend that I realized women could be just as dirty as men. None of the girls who worked there were trying to talk to me before. But now that I had a girlfriend, they were all into me. It was flat out ridiculous! One chick, with whom I'd been a little interested prior to being with Ebony was the worst. Anytime Ebony wasn't around, she flirted and groped me. I couldn't believe it. She hadn't shown me the time of day before. Aside from working there, she was also an exotic dancer, with the perfect shape. She went out of the way to ask me questions like, "How do my pants fit?" or "Can you see my bra through my shirt?" I'd just walk away.

One day, as I was leaving to go home, she came running out to my car. I rolled my window down and asked, "What's up?"

"I want you to see the new belly chain I just bought." She pulled down her shorts a little so I could see the chain.

I could see not only the chain but her waist and some of her butt, too. The sight was wonderful, but I backed my car up and pulled off.

She blew me a kiss and said, "You know you want it!"

Yes, I did, but she was too late. I learned to stay away from her. She was too tempting, and I knew if I continued to flirt with fire, I would get burned. She wasn't the only girl working there who flirted with me, but she was the most persistent. I knew her game. She just wanted me because I belonged to someone else. The moment I slipped and went after her, she would've let me go. Some people just want what they can't have. I was happy with my girlfriend.

Another girl was interested in me as well. She also worked at the Blue Crab as a hostess, and her name was Dionne. She worked alongside Ebony. She had never shown any interest in me either until she noticed that Ebony liked me. Before Ebony and I were a couple, she and I had exchanged telephone numbers, and she began calling me right away. She was cute but too clingy. Once, we were talking on the phone, and she asked me for the name of the apartment complex where I lived. After I told her, she hung up. I tried calling her back, but she didn't answer.

About twenty minutes later, she called me from a different number. "I'm at a payphone inside your apartment complex," she said. "Which building do you live in?"

At first, I didn't believe her, but she put me on hold. As I held on, I heard a car horn honking loudly.

She came back on the phone. "Did you hear the horn honking?"

"Was that you?"

"Yes. Now, which building?"

I told her, and she came by. We talked for a few minutes and started watching a movie. Five minutes into the movie, she turned to me and said, "Let's have sex."

I was taken aback, but I agreed. The only problem was I didn't have a condom. I told her about my dilemma.

"Don't worry about it," she said.

"Hang on. I'm going to run to the gas station."

"Don't go to the gas station. Let's just have sex!"

I thought she was kidding. I left her at my place and drove to the gas station at about 100 miles per hour. When I returned to my place, she was pissed.

"I have a condom!" I said.

"I don't like condoms! You're not going to put that on."

Although I wanted to have sex, I wasn't about to do it without a condom.

"Fine, then!" she snapped. She grabbed her keys and left.

I was dumbfounded. I thought the chick was crazy. I told myself I was going to leave her alone and kick it with Ebony.

I was glad I had decided to stick with Ebony. Dionne ended up hanging out with one of the other guys we worked with. He told me what had occurred between them, and he was mad at me for not warning him about her.

"Dude, this chick is crazy!" he said.

She had pulled the same no-condom move with him. He said they'd had sex once, but when he tried to bring a condom to bed again, she got upset and left.

Dionne abruptly stopped working at the Blue Crab. A few months later, she came to the restaurant to have lunch, and she was pregnant. The other guy and I laughed when we saw her. We were laughing to keep from crying, relieved we had avoided a serious blow. We weren't sure if she was trying to get pregnant or if she was already pregnant and hoping to trap one of us into thinking the baby was ours. Either way, we had dodged a bullet!

Although my girlfriend and I were happy with each other, her parents weren't. I guess we were spending too much time together. Her dad was the pastor of a church, and her mom was the first lady. It seemed the rumors about church girls were true. Ebony was freaky. Her mom was cool with me, but her dad never had two words to say to me. I got it, I was dating his only child, his little girl. Her dad was much older than her mom. He worked two jobs, and he was hardly ever home. However, when he *was* home, I was usually there as well. It didn't take me long to get the hint. He didn't want me around. I told Ebony she needed to start coming over to my place more, but she still wouldn't come over that much. I soon realized why. Once, when she was over, I went to take the trash out, and I noticed her dad sitting in his truck a few buildings down. He was keeping an eye on her—or me. I was shocked. Ebony was almost twenty years old! When I went back into my apartment, I laughed and told Ebony I had just seen her dad. She panicked, grabbed her things, and told me she had to go.

She later told me her dad was overprotective, and it would be a good idea if I just came over to her place. I told her to stop being so afraid of her dad.

"I'm his only child, and you should respect that," she chided.

"Whatever." I wasn't going to tiptoe around her dad.

I stopped going over her house so much, partially to prove a point. I only went once a week. She called me every day to come over, but I told her I was busy. She started to feel frustrated, so she started coming to my place every morning before she went to her first class. I was cool with that. At least she was trying.

Since she was trying, I began going back over her place more often. One evening, her dad must've been off work. I knew it as soon as I pulled into the driveway and saw his white truck. When I rang the doorbell, he came to the door. I said hello and he told me to come in. Ebony was standing in the foyer. He told her to step out of the room and let him and I talk for a while. She just stood there.

"Don't make me repeat myself!" he warned.

She scampered off like she usually did. I wasn't worried about him, but I was pissed that she let her daddy intimidate her so badly. He asked me to take a seat. As soon as I did, the first lady walked into the room also. He immediately started grilling me, while his wife sat there quietly. I guess they were used to him running things.

He asked me, "What do you want with my daughter?"

"I just like her, and we're dating," I replied.

"You're a bad influence on her. You're spending too much time together. She barely goes to school, and when she does, she stops at your place first. My daughter is no Jezebel. You need to stay away from her."

I was respectful, but I advised him that I had no intentions to stop seeing his daughter. "If you don't want me to come to your house any longer, I won't; however, I am not going to stop Ebony from coming to see me. Yes, Ebony does come by every morning, but that is by her own free will. I have never disrespected Ebony or you and your wife, and I never will."

He became upset at my audacity to speak up to him. "Young man, who do you think you're talking to?"

"I mean no disrespect, but I'm speaking to you. This is a conversation you need to have with your daughter, not me." As I turned around to leave, his wife finally spoke.

"I apologize for the way my husband was yelling at you. He is just protective of his little girl. All he wants is for her to focus on school. She's only eighteen years old and just graduated from high school. School should be her focus, not boys."

"I understand, but—" I stopped and thought about what she'd said. "Did you mean to say twenty years old?"

"No, I know how old my child is! Let me guess, she told you she was older?"

"Yes, ma'am. She told me she's twenty."

"No, honey. She is only eighteen!"

I was pissed off at Ebony. Why had she lied to me? I didn't talk to her for a week. I now understood her dad. I was just glad he didn't try to shoot me. I still dated Ebony for a while, but I wasn't sure if I could trust her.

As time went on, Ebony stopped hosting and started serving, and I found myself working side by side with her, often in the same section. I couldn't stand it, because, now, I wasn't only looking after my tables but hers as well. And it didn't help that she wouldn't stop being freaky at work. Every opportunity she had to grope me, she would. I hated working with her because she wasn't a great server, either.

Veronica started giving me a lot of duties. I didn't know it, but she was slowly grooming me to take over a leadership role. I became a trainer for new servers. When there was outside training to be done, Veronica always sent me to be the liaison for our location. I started traveling locally with the managers for company initiatives. I liked the additional responsibilities. Whenever the corporate people came into town, Veronica always had me waiting on them. I found it harder and harder to work with my girlfriend, who didn't have the highest standards for serving.

Liar Liar

Ebony didn't stay at the Blue Crab much longer because Veronica fired her. Although Veronica and I were close, I was angry with her for firing my girlfriend. I had worked the lunch shift on the day she was fired. Ebony was coming in to work the dinner shift. As soon as she walked in, Veronica asked Ebony and two other servers, a girl and a guy, to come to the office with her. Veronica had also asked the hostess not to seat guests at their tables.

They must've been in the office for about an hour. I didn't know what was going on. After the hour was up, the three servers, including Ebony, walked out of the office. Ebony and the other girl looked as if they had been crying, and the guy looked like he was about to drop a tear at any moment. All three of them grabbed their things and left. I tried to talk to Ebony, but she said she had to leave immediately.

After Ebony left, I tried to talk to Veronica. "Veronica, what happened?"

"I can't talk about it, Carter. It's confidential."

"Was Ebony just fired?" I pressed.

"You'll have to talk to Ebony about that."

As soon as my shift was over, I called Ebony and asked her to stop by my place. She said sure but didn't come by for another two hours. When she came over, she tried to get freaky with me, like I was going to forget what had happened at work. I stopped her immediately and asked her about it.

"Veronica let me, Rico, and Tasha go," she said.

"For what reason?"

"Veronica accused us of stealing."

"What did you steal?"

"I didn't steal anything!" she said, offended.

"Well, you shouldn't let Veronica just fire you when you didn't do anything wrong."

"Just let it go. I was tired of working there anyway."

I couldn't believe how nonchalant she was. "You can't just let it go. You should contact the corporate office and complain," I suggested. "Even if you don't want your job back, you should at least clear your name."

"It isn't worth it anymore. Just let it go."

I couldn't let it go, and I eventually convinced Ebony to call corporate. I gave her the number, and she said she was going to go into the other room and call. After about twenty minutes, she came out of the room and said she was on hold too long. She promised she would call back and said she wouldn't let it go. I was fine with that answer.

When I went back to work the next day, I had nothing to say to Veronica. For her to be a stand-up manager, I was appalled that she had terminated Ebony like that. I guess Veronica felt the tension. She asked me to come to the office. For a moment, I thought she was going to fire me as well. I wasn't scared, though, because I knew I had done nothing wrong. *Bring it on!* I thought.

When I got to the office, she asked me if I had talked to Ebony. I told her I had.

"What did you find out?" she asked.

"I found out you fired her for no reason."

Veronica rolled her eyes. "She didn't tell you she and the other two servers were stealing?"

I was in disbelief, and I let her know. "There's no way Ebony would steal anything!"

Veronica almost laughed at me, but she maintained her composure, raising her eyebrow. "Let me show you!" She explained to me that Sean had gone on vacation and hadn't been in the restaurant for over a week. "Do you know how the managers' blue cards work?"

"Yes, if a customer doesn't like the food or if they changed their mind, the manager uses the blue card to take the items off the bill."

"Exactly."

I still had no idea what this had to do with Ebony and, better yet, Sean.

As if reading my mind, Veronica went into detail. "Sean hasn't worked in over a week. He must've dropped his card or forgot it when he went on vacation. Well, someone picked it up, either Ebony, Rico, or Tasha."

"How could you know that?"

She had me look at the computer. She explained that the computer tracked each time a manager swiped the card and for what reason. She showed me that although Sean had not been in the building for over a week, his card had been used every day that he'd been off. The card had only been used between three servers: Ebony, Rico, and Tasha. She explained they had been passing around Sean's card on their shifts. Every time a customer paid their bill with cash, the three of them used Sean's card to void the transaction and keep the cash for themselves.

I was still skeptical, unconvinced that Ebony would do something like that.

Veronica sensed that I still didn't believe her. She said, "Carter, you should ask Ebony about it. She already confessed to scamming the Blue Crab. The only reason I didn't press charges was because of you. I know you're upset, but the truth is Ebony stole from the Blue Crab, whether you believe it or not."

I knew Veronica was telling the truth, but I still didn't want to believe Ebony had anything to do with it. Surely, she was set up. I wanted to get to the bottom of it. Tasha stayed in the same apartment complex as me, and I knew where Rico lived because I had dropped him off at home before. As soon as I got off work, I went straight over to Rico's house. I asked him what happened, and he told me they'd gotten caught stealing.

"How did you get Ebony involved?" I asked.

He laughed at me as he lit his cigarette. "Ebony is the one who brought the scam to me and Tasha. You need to go check your woman." He was acting confrontational like he wanted to fight. As I was leaving, he said, "Don't come back over here with that bullshit!"

I started to turn around and confront him for saying that to me, but I thought better of it and left. Rico and I had been cool up until that moment. It wasn't worth it to get into an altercation.

As soon as I left his place, I went to talk to Tasha. She confirmed what he had said, that Ebony had brought the scam up to them. She was disappointed that she had gotten caught up in the scheme but said she wanted to move on. She was just happy Veronica didn't press charges.

I still couldn't believe it. There was no way Ebony would've done this. Surely, both Rico and Tasha were lying. Next, I went to Ebony's house. As soon as I pulled up, I saw that her mom and dad were home. I didn't want to go in, but I had to get to the bottom of this. Someone was lying on Ebony, and I didn't think it was fair to her. This time, Ebony's mom answered the door. I still had on my Blue Crab uniform.

Her mom let me in. "I can't believe you still work at that place!"

"Why do you say that?" I asked.

"Ebony was right for quitting. I can't believe the managers let the customers curse Ebony out without doing anything about it. Ebony came home crying, and she told me the manager was standing right there when that man put his finger in my child's face and cursed her out. I asked her did they make the guy leave, and Ebony said no. They just got him another server. Her dad and I were about to go up there, but Ebony begged us not to. She said she was going to call the corporate office on the manager up there. Do you know anything about it?"

I shook my head. "No, I don't." It was clear now. Ebony was a compulsive liar and a thief. I wished her parents would've gone up to the Blue Crab and spoken with Veronica. They would've been in for the shock of their lives.

I knew I could never trust Ebony, but we continued to date, more for convenience than anything else.

Payday

Veronica had her hands full. Ebony's theft wasn't the last occurrence she had to deal with. Every Friday, the entire team received their paychecks. This was before direct deposit. The checks would always come hand delivered by UPS by nine a.m. A manager folded the checks and put them in an alphabetized folder. When the crew arrived, they stopped by the office and picked up their checks. Sometimes, the managers would get too busy to pass out the checks, so they'd give the folder to a trusted team member to pass them out.

Prior to Veronica taking over, picking up the checks would sometimes be a disaster. People would walk in at any time to pick up their checks, causing chaos. They would often get upset because they had to wait for a manager to make time to get their checks. Some of the workers would leave once they realized the manager was too busy, and they'd come back later but still couldn't get their checks.

Veronica established parameters. She only allowed people to come at two different times on Friday: between three and four p.m. and between ten and eleven p.m. If we came in at any other time, we could forget about getting our checks. She wasn't going to let anything disrupt the business. Because the checks were folded and sealed already, she had the takeout cashier give out the checks when we came to pick them up. We had to sign off to show we had received it. The takeout cashier would also go around and pass out the checks to the team members that were working that day. This process worked out a whole lot better.

At first, team members tested out this new method. They still attempted to come in at any time to pick their checks up. They complained that the checks got there at nine a.m., so they shouldn't have to wait to pick them up, but Veronica would not budge on her new policy. Once people knew she was serious, they simply came at the appropriate time.

One Friday, the new process turned into a complete and utter disaster. The checks had come in from UPS at the usual scheduled time of nine a.m. Several other UPS deliveries came in as well. Sean was the manager that morning, and he was swamped. He signed off for the checks and put them in the office. He proceeded to check in the other deliveries as well. The produce was the first check-in. When the produce came, the manager was automatically stuck at the door, checking in every case that came in. Usually, the produce delivery person had to do anywhere between four and six loads before the drop off was complete. Often, the manager was stuck at the door for about ten minutes. After completing the produce check-in, Sean had to do the liquor as well, checking in each bottle. Dealing with the deliveries put him behind by almost twenty minutes.

Once he was done, he wanted to begin the process of folding the checks and putting them away. The only problem was Sean couldn't find the checks. He first thought he had misplaced them. He looked everywhere for the checks, in the safe, the file cabinet, and he even went to the backdoor to see if he'd left them there. He started to panic slightly, but he knew they would show up. He just had to remember where he'd put them.

It was close to opening time. Sean decided to check in the

servers and go unlock the front door for opening. It still bothered him that he couldn't find the checks.

Once the next manager came in, he asked her to help him find the checks. Because she knew the severity of the situation, she began to help. They both tore the office up, looking for them. When they couldn't find the checks, they had no choice but to call Veronica and tell her what happened. In a few hours, people would be coming in to pick up their checks, and there would be a riot if they couldn't get paid.

Veronica verified with Sean that he had, indeed, received the checks, and she told him she was on the way up there. She searched every nook and cranny of the office as well as the entire restaurant. When she couldn't find the checks, she immediately called the director of operations, and he advised her to contact corporate security to get ahead of the problem.

Corporate security canceled every check immediately and went into investigation mode. Within a couple of hours, they contacted Veronica and advised that they had located the checks. Several of them had already been cashed at the check cashing place down the street from the restaurant. Veronica thought that was impossible because no one had picked up their checks yet. They advised her they'd verified that the checks were dropped off at the Blue Crab and signed off by Sean, but someone in the restaurant must've gotten to the checks and started cashing them. Corporate asked her to provide the entire roster for that location. They were going to do some more digging and get back to her shortly. She stopped them before they hung up and asked them, "What about the employees who haven't received their checks? What can be done about that?" They told her to contact her director. They were only in charge of security, which meant that part was on her to handle. Unfortunately for Veronica, she had a restaurant full of disgruntled employees, waiting for their checks. Some of them had already called the corporate office and the area director themselves.

Within an hour, corporate security already had the police

dispatched to the check cashing company. Luckily, the company had cameras. After about thirty minutes, they were able to produce a recording of someone attempting to cash an entire bundle of Blue Crab checks. The person had produced identification. However, once the police ran the ID, they quickly realized it was fake. Although the information on the ID was false, the picture matched the person on the recording. The police brought the recording to the Blue Crab and explained to Veronica that they had video footage of the person cashing the checks but not a matching name. They wanted to show the managers and employees the recording to see if anyone recognized the individual. The police asked if we had a VHS and television. We had both. The Blue Crab used the television and recorder for training purposes.

As soon as the video started, everyone surrounded the television, curious about who had stolen our money. It only took thirty seconds into the recording for us all to recognize the culprit. As soon as he walked into the check cashing place, we could see his face clearly plastered on the screen.

Like a choir, everyone shouted in unison, "Ant!"

We were all shocked that someone who worked there had stolen the checks. We thought that maybe Sean had left the checks sitting out in the dining room and a customer picked them up, or maybe the UPS driver had stolen them, not someone who worked side by side with us every day.

One of the employees said, "Yo, I got this one!" and started to walk out of the building.

The police stopped him immediately and advised him to let them handle it.

Someone else yelled, "He sells weed, too. You'll probably find it on him or in his car."

The police did a great job settling everyone down and advised they would do their best to get Ant into custody ASAP. They also, once again, advised everyone to leave it in the hands of the authorities.

A few hours later, the police contacted Veronica and told her they had Ant in custody. His dumb ass was still out there trying to cash checks at other check cashing companies. What Ant didn't know was that his picture was sent to all banks and check cashing companies within a ten-mile radius. They were all advised to contact the authorities if they saw him.

They caught up with Ant, sitting in the lobby of a check cashing company two miles away from the Blue Crab. He was asleep with all the checks still on him, stuffed into his jacket pocket. They also found some bags of weed on him. They said they could hardly wake him up. He was so high from his own supply that he was in a stupor.

I'm not sure how much time Ant spent in jail, but he'd better be glad the police found him and not some of the people that worked at the Blue Crab.

The Blue Crab did a good job of getting everyone their money. After canceling all the checks, they had them reissued the following morning. Most of the employees were happy, but a few tried to get more from the company. They stated that they had to pay late fees on some of their bills that had been due that Friday. Their tactic didn't work, however.

I'm not sure what happened to Sean afterward. I don't know if he ever made it to working in the corporate office or if he was fired for his mishap, but we never saw him again after that day. It was said that he'd transferred out of state, but I think he was terminated.

Homesick

I wouldn't stay in Georgia much longer. It had been three years, and I was homesick. When I told Veronica how I felt, she was sad to see me go, but she wanted what was best for me. She told me to let her know which Blue Crab I wanted to go back to in Michigan, and she would contact the general manager to transfer me. I told her where I wanted to go, but she said she wouldn't transfer me there because it wasn't a good location, and I would never make any money. I wanted to go there because it was closest to my dad's house. I was going to be living upstairs from my dad when I went back home. It didn't matter to Veronica, though. She refused to transfer me to that location. She told me which restaurant she was going to contact. She knew the general manager well and said it would be a great location for me.

I was ready to get back home, but my lease wasn't ending for another month and a half. Although I was never interested in having a roommate, I decided to help one of the guys who worked there with me. He was a cool guy, so when he told me he had just lost his place and needed somewhere to stay, I let him move in with me. It was no big deal. We had hung out before and had drinks, and I figured a month and a half wouldn't be bad.

Well, I couldn't have been more wrong. His name was Kwame, and he was the biggest weed head ever. I hadn't been around someone who smoked weed since I was in college. I had dabbled slightly back in my college days but quickly gave it up, but Kwame stayed high. I don't think he was able to cope without smoking weed, and he always kept weed on him . If he was at work, he had the weed in his pocket. I often wondered why he went to the bathroom so much. It was so he could take quick hits. He said he only took a couple of puffs to get him through, and no one seemed to notice that the bathroom always smelled like weed when he came out.

I started to ask Kwame to leave my apartment. I didn't want to be affiliated with him and his weed. However, I knew it was going to be only five or six weeks, so I decided to live with it. As long as it didn't affect me, I was good. He wasn't carrying any weight or distributing weed, so I shrugged it off.

Kwame asked me if we could have a party at my place. I shut that down quickly. I envisioned all the weed heads we worked with and the ones I didn't know, crowding my place, tearing it up with smoke everywhere. Kwame was disappointed I had said no, but I didn't care.

He even started asking me if he could use my car. Once again, I shut that down. The last thing I needed was Kwame getting pulled over while driving my car with weed on his person. Or, better yet, getting in an accident because he was high. No thank you!

It had only been a week since Kwame became my roommate, and we already didn't like each other. I found myself working more or just staying out of the apartment because I simply didn't want to be around him. I couldn't believe someone else was keeping me from staying at my own place. I also started to see why he'd lost his place. He was filthy, and he didn't like to work. I guess smoking all that weed made him lazy. The dude wouldn't wash a dish to save his life. I was working almost sixty hours a week, and he was barely getting in twenty hours. The math was easy: Working part-time, plus smoking plenty of weed equaled no money to pay bills. For guys like him, it was easier to live off people than to grow up and face responsibilities. If I had planned to stay longer, he would've had to get out.

It didn't help that he had to go see his probation officer every week. Although I had told him on multiple occasions that he couldn't use my car, he still asked as if we'd never spoken about it before. He wanted to play stupid, but I wasn't stupid. I said no to him with no hesitation. He figured if he kept asking to use my car, I would eventually give in and say yes. What he didn't realize was the more he asked me, the more it pissed me off and made it easier for me to just say no! I don't get people like that. They have no shame. I would rather work for what I need than continuously ask for favors. Kwame had no problem with it. And why did he have to see a probation officer? Because he had gotten pulled over with a nice amount of weed and paraphernalia on him. I wondered why he told me that if he wanted to use my car. He was stupid. And he thought I was stupid as well.

I continued to work heavy hours as I prepared to move back to Michigan. I wanted to make as much money as I could to make the move easier. I wasn't going to take anything with me on my move back home, except for my clothes and my television. Kwame asked if he could have my bed and furniture. I told him that would be no problem. That way, I didn't have to worry about throwing it out myself.

As the time to go back home drew nearer, I noticed that Kwame wasn't making any plans to move out. The week prior to my move, he asked if I could extend my lease so he could stay there. He promised he would send me the money every month, and I could send a check in my name to pay the lease. I told him no. I don't think I'd said yes to anything he asked of me other than the furniture. Everything he asked was a dumb question. I should've said no to him moving in with me in the first place. He had an attitude with me for saying no and, once again, I couldn't care less.

As we approached the last five days prior to my move, Kwame hadn't packed a bag or anything. I asked him what his plans were, and he said he didn't know. He would just stay there until they kicked him out. I told him I wasn't cool with him doing that because it would prevent me from getting my security deposit back, and I was counting on that money. I also asked him about the furniture and what his plan was to get it out of there. He didn't know. He was getting agitated by all my questions. The dude was acting like I was staying at his place or something.

I bluffed him and told him someone wanted to buy my furniture for five hundred dollars, and they were going to be coming by to look at it and take it with them.

"Please, man," he begged, "don't let them buy the furniture. I really need it!"

"I just can't let the furniture stay here without any certainty it'll be gone. I have to do a walkthrough with the apartment leasing agents, and the apartment has to be clean and clear," I explained.

"Please! I can have someone come by and take it in two days."

Two days later, I was about to head off to work, and there was still no one there to get the furniture. I advised Kwame that I was going to sell it if I came back home and the furniture was still there.

I worked the entire day, and when I got home, the furniture was still there. I was pissed. "I'm going to call the other people and sell the furniture," I warned. Truthfully, I was going to risk putting it on the curb. No one wanted to buy it, but I knew the furniture had to be out prior to the walkthrough.

The next morning, I woke Kwame up early. "The buyers will be here in an hour to get the furniture," I said. "And they're going to take the bed you're sleeping on, too."

"Where am I going to sleep?"

The audacity! I wanted to say, "Outside, with the rest of the homeless people." Instead, I said, "Look Kwame, I am moving out in two days, and I have to get the furniture and *you* out of here before I leave. The people are on the way with five hundred dollars. I don't care where you sleep, but I need that bed."

He finally realized I was leaving, and he had to go. "Look, man, I really need that furniture. My homeboy said I can move in with him if I bring that furniture because he doesn't have any. I have three hundred dollars on me that you can have right now, but please call those people back and let me keep the furniture."

I thought he was lying, but he reached into his pocket and gave me three crisp one-hundred-dollar bills.

"I can have it out of here today," he promised.

"This is putting me in a bind, but I'll take your money as long as it's out of here today."

To my surprise, his new sucker of a roommate came by with a U-Haul truck and picked up the furniture. I thought Kwame was going to go with him, but he stayed. I guess he was going to stay until I turned the keys in. I envisioned him standing right outside the door in his underwear, with a sleeping bag under his arm and a suitcase as I turned the keys over to the leasing agent. He made me sick.

My last day of work had arrived, and I was going to work the day shift only and pack my car up at night, so I could hit the road to Michigan the next morning. Veronica had already taken care of everything for my transfer. I just had to go talk to my new GM the following Monday. I didn't have to be at work until eleven a.m., but I was up early. I was excited about moving back home.

Kwame knocked on my bedroom door at around eight o'clock in the morning. I asked him what he needed.

"Can you take me to see my probation officer?"

"Yeah, I can, but we need to leave now because I have to be at work at eleven." Although he was irritating, I wasn't going to let him bother me on the last day. I figured I would do him that last favor, and I would never see him again for the rest of my life. It was still early enough for me to get him to his probation officer and back to my place, so I decided not to put my work clothes on until I came back.

We got ready quickly, and I asked him where we were going, which was stupid. I should've asked him before I had agreed to take him. He told me it was an hour drive. I was furious! He saw that I was angry, but he assured me we could be there by nine thirty and back by ten thirty. But he still had to meet with the probation officer, and he didn't seem to be accounting for the time that would take.

Kwame said, "Nah, dude, I just have to drop, and that's it."

I knew drop meant he had to give a urine sample to make sure he was clean. I gave him a look. I had just seen him smoking a few days ago. I couldn't believe he was going to walk into his probation meeting and pee in a cup, knowing he was going to fail.

As if he knew what I was thinking, he said, "I'm good."

"No way you're good. I just saw you smoke three days ago."

"Trust me, dude. I do this all the time. I drink Golden Seal forty-eight hours prior to the drug test, and it flushes my system out and makes me drop clean. Drinking that stuff and a couple of gallons of water have me peeing out of control, but it works." He also explained that the police station used urine for their tests, not hair follicles like most chemists used.

I was amazed that he knew about the standardization of drug testing but couldn't use his mind for anything else. I just wanted to make sure I wasn't walking into something. I didn't want to get arrested for driving the stupid guy to a drug test that he couldn't pass. I didn't know if they were going to say I was guilty by association or being an accomplice.

I wanted to get him to the probation office and back quickly. I didn't want to be late on my last day at work. Veronica had done a lot for me, so I didn't want to let her down. I believed in giving a hundred percent all the way to the end. As we were driving, I noticed I was going a little too fast, but I was hurrying. We were in an area I had never seen before, the countryside of Georgia. I wanted to get there and back as quickly as possible. The faster I went, the closer I would be to never seeing Kwame again.

We had been driving for almost an hour when Kwame said

we were getting closer. After a few more miles, he told me I was at the exit. I turned on my right turn signal and started veering into the exit lane. Just as I was merging onto the ramp, Kwame said, "My bad. This isn't the exit."

I still had time, so I quickly put my left turn signal on and veered out. I noticed a police car was doing the same thing behind me. I knew instantly they were following us. I didn't realize when I had jumped lanes, they were already trailing us. I knew they thought I was trying to lose them. Had I known they were behind me, I wouldn't have jumped the lane.

I told Kwame, "Don't look, but the police are trailing us."

Of course, he snapped his head back to look. I kept driving, making sure I was going the speed limit. They kept following me. Two exits up, Kwame said we were at the right exit. I asked him if he was sure, and he said yes. I made sure I turned on my right turn signal and slowly merged onto the exit lane. I was hoping the police would keep going forward on the freeway but, nope, they turned on their right turn signal and merged as well. Once we got off the exit ramp, Kwame told me to turn left. We were stuck at the light, and the police were right behind us. As the light turned green, I put my left turn signal on and turned left. For the first time since they'd been trailing us, they didn't do the same thing. They did something worse. They turned their police lights on. I was hoping they wouldn't pull us over, that they had already run my license plate and tags and realized the car hadn't been reported stolen. Unfortunately, we were in Georgia with Michigan plates, and we were two young, black men in our early twenties. We were being profiled.

I turned on my right turn signal and pulled over to the right side of the embankment. As we sat there, I asked Kwame if he had any weed on him. He told me he didn't, but I didn't believe him. I was worried. We sat, waiting for the police officer to come over to the car, but he just sat there, flashing his lights on us for what seemed like five minutes. Kwame was getting impatient and said he was about to get out and talk to the officer himself.

"No!" I commanded. "You are not going to get out of this car! You are going to sit here and wait."

As we waited for the officer to come up to the car, two more police cars pulled up. He had been waiting on back up to arrive as if we'd just escaped prison or something.

Now that the police officer had two backups, he finally got out of the police cruiser and approached my vehicle. He was on my side, and another officer approached on Kwame's side. The other two officers remained standing outside of their cruiser. I asked Kwame one last time if he was clean, and he said he was.

As they drew closer, I slowly placed my hands on the steering wheel. The officer came up to my window and asked for my license and registration. I told him it was in my back pocket and asked if I could reach back there and get it. He told me I could as he kept an eagle eye on my every movement. When I produced the proper documents, he seemed a little surprised.

He asked me, "Where are you going?"

"I'm just taking a friend to his probation appointment," I replied.

"Why did you swerve out of the lane when you noticed we were behind you?"

"I didn't swerve because you were behind me. I swerved out of the lane because we were at the wrong exit."

I could tell he didn't believe me. "Is it okay if I check the car?"

I told him it was okay. I was relieved I had never let Kwame or anyone else use my car. I knew there was no drugs or anything else illegal in my vehicle.

The officer asked us to step out of the vehicle and step to the back. He told us to place our hands on the vehicle as the officers began searching us. After finding nothing on us, they advised us that they were going to put us in handcuffs while they searched. I wanted to ensure that we were not under arrest, and he told us we weren't. The handcuffs were precautionary, to protect us and them. They proceeded to handcuff us and had us sit on the railing on the side of the road.

I was outraged and embarrassed. I noticed that one of the police cars had K-9 Unit on the side panel. As if he realized I was looking at the K-9 vehicle, one of the officers opened the door and out came a large German Shepard. They first walked the dog around the car for a few minutes. Then they put the dog inside my car. After a while, they pulled the dog out. I saw one of the officer's shrug at the other and mouth, "Nothing."

The initial officer, who had pulled us over, wasn't satisfied with that answer, so he decided to search the car himself. He was determined to find something on us. I started to get nervous, thinking he may try to plant something in the car. Kwame looked at me and said, "This is some bullshit right here." For the first time in a while, I agreed with him. It *was* some bullshit.

The officer diligently searched my vehicle. He took apart pieces of my car I hadn't even realized came apart. At one point, my glove compartment was sitting on top of my car. He took apart every cupholder and vent, looking for drugs.

One of the other officers casually walked over to him as he was inspecting my vehicle with a fine-tooth comb and whispered something to him. The officer turned red, either from embarrassment for being called out for being biased during a basic traffic stop or because he couldn't find anything on us. Nevertheless, he reluctantly walked over to us and told us we were free to go. I was careful not to laugh at them for wasting their time. I didn't want them to find a way to arrest us for something else.

As soon as we got back into the car, I very carefully pulled away from the cops. We were just down the street from Kwame's probation officer. We pulled in, and Kwame hopped out and said he would be back in a few minutes. I had lost track of time. It was already ten thirty! We were pulled over for an entire hour, dealing with that bullshit. I was pissed. I was supposed to be at work in a half hour, but I was over an hour away from my job. It didn't help that I wasn't even in uniform yet. And, of course, Kwame was in the building for almost twenty minutes. Part of me wanted to just pull off and leave him there. I was about to do that when he came walking out of the office. He had the nerve to be mad because they'd had him waiting. Of course, it was all about him. He never once apologized to me for messing up my day. It was now eleven a.m. and I was officially late for work.

Although I wanted to drive back to my place at one hundred miles per hour, I was careful to follow the speed limit and all other traffic laws. I was not going to risk being pulled over again. Kwame tried to talk to me, but I had no conversation for him. I was less than twenty-four hours away from never seeing him again. Despite being angry, the thought of Kwame going away made me smile a little.

Traffic was tight, which made things worse. I didn't make it back to my place until almost twelve thirty. I quickly got dressed and headed to work, two hours late on my last shift.

When I got to work, I hurriedly made it inside, and the first people I saw were Veronica and the hostess. The hostess was standing there with an attitude, but Veronica looked relieved and concerned. She asked me if I was okay. She knew something was wrong because I would never do her like that. I told her everything that happened, and she said she was happy I was okay.

We were already done with the lunch rush, so Veronica asked me if I still wanted to stay or just be done. I told her I wanted to work, even if it was for just a few hours. She let me stay, and it was slow. The last table I served at that location asked me for a pitcher of water and a lot of lemons. I hurried back and got them what they wanted. A lot of people liked to put lemon in their water; however, this wasn't the case for them. When I came back to the table, they proceeded to make lemonade. They had gone around and took all the sugar packets off the empty tables. Some people had no shame. At that point, I was ready to go. I asked Veronica if she still needed me, and she said I could leave after I finished that table.

Once my last table left, I cleaned up and was ready to cash out all my money. As I was cashing out, Veronica came by and said she wanted to talk to me in the back room before I left. I assured her I wasn't going to leave without first saying goodbye to everyone. Once I had collected my money, I proceeded to the backroom. Veronica was already back there waiting for me, but to my surprise, so was the rest of the crew. They had balloons, cake, and gifts for me. Everyone had signed a big card that read "Wish You Luck." They'd also bought me a baseball jersey that had #1 Team Player written on the front and my name on the back. Everyone gave me hugs and kisses and told me they hated to see me leave. I got a little choked up about the entire ordeal. I had no idea I meant that much to everyone. Even Veronica, who had nerves of steel, was crying. She said she was going to miss me a bunch. Through her tears, she told me my transfer was complete, and all I had to do was go to the Blue Crab in Michigan on Monday. She said the general manager was a good friend of hers, and he would be expecting me.

 I hurried and left the restaurant, a little embarrassed that I had gotten choked up before leaving. I drove straight to my apartment, so I could tell Kwame to hit the road. I wanted to finish packing without distractions. When entering my apartment, I noticed Kwame was gone and had left the key on the kitchen counter. I was overjoyed that I never had to see him again. It didn't surprise me that he took some other things that didn't belong to him, and it didn't bother me at all. That meant less packing for me. I was just glad he was gone. I immediately started packing the remainder of the things I had. I was ready to hit the road at five o'clock in the morning.

MOVING BACK NORTH

I WAS ELATED TO MOVE BACK UP NORTH. I WAS BACK IN MY ELEMENT, with Michigan's much faster pace. The South was a little too laid back for me. No one was *ever* in a hurry. Most importantly, this was where my family and true friends were.

I got to Michigan at around five o'clock in the evening. I first saw my mom and dad and went to see some of my friends. I had never developed any true friends in the South, more so just friends by association or coworkers. I hung out with my friends all evening on Saturday and my family all day on Sunday. It was the best!

I wasn't on the schedule for Monday at the Blue Crab, but Veronica had set an appointment for me to meet with the general manager, Sal, at ten o'clock in the morning. He wanted to meet with me first to go over the standards of his restaurant and make sure we were on the same page. I made sure to put on a shirt, tie, and dress pants to meet with him. I wanted to make a good impression on Sal.

As I drove up to the restaurant, I was immediately impressed with the area. I had never been out there before. It was a great location, just outside a popular, ritzy mall. I made sure I was fifteen minutes early for my meeting. Once I got to the restaurant, Sal met me at the back door. He had on a Hawaiian polo shirt, and he wore a gold necklace and a gold watch. He reminded me of one of those smooth Italian gangsters from the movies. He invited me into the restaurant and had me wait for him in the dining room while he finished up some things.

As I sat there waiting, I saw a familiar person walk past me. It was Kareem, the cook from the Blue Crab where I had previously worked, Miyah's ex-boyfriend.

He saw me and gave the standard Detroit greeting. "What up doe?" He gave me some dap. "What are you doing here?"

"I'm here to meet with Sal. I'm transferring here from Georgia."

"Are you a manager now, or something?"

"Nah, I'm not a manager."

He tried to put me on blast for dressing up like I was a manager. It didn't bother me that he was trying to clown me. I had no interest in being like him, so his opinion didn't matter. Kareem told me there were five people from the old Blue Crab crew still working there. Most of them were in the kitchen. Ciara was one of them. I had forgotten all about her, although I'd told her I would stay in touch.

Sal came out of the kitchen and saw Kareem and me talking. It looked as if he was second-guessing me because I knew Kareem. Great, I was guilty by association. I could already tell Kareem was a pain in the ass.

Sal sat down with me and went over his expectations for the restaurant and me. He told me I came highly recommended from Veronica and asked when I was available to start.

"I can start tomorrow," I said.

"I'm going to put you with another server, so you can shadow for a couple of shifts, to see if you can handle the pace."

I thought, *Really, dude?* If Veronica had already recommended me, he should've known I was qualified. But I didn't say anything.

I kept my mouth shut and decided to show him my worth instead of talking about it.

The next day, I came in early and helped set the kitchen up with my training server. That was helpful, so I could know where everything was located. After we set up the kitchen, my trainer sat down with me and started going over the menu. I knew the answers to all her questions. She agreed that I knew the menu, and there was no need for me to follow her. She told me she would follow me for the first hour just to see how I did on my own. It was going to be a piece of cake for me because I knew how to serve. Sal was acting like I was new to the company. I had just worked less than forty-eight hours ago for the same company in a different state. But I remained quiet and did what I was told. I was new to their restaurant and had asked to be there (somewhat), so I obliged.

My trainer was given a table, and she told me to go ahead and greet them as if I were the server, and she would stand back and observe. She could've gone home for all I cared because I didn't need to be observed. She quickly realized that as well. After I had taken the first three tables, she went up to Sal and said I didn't need any training at all. I was good to go. Sal asked if she was sure, and she confirmed. I was relieved. I didn't have time to go through training for something I already knew how to do.

I made good money on my first shift. The guests were polite and easy to deal with. They could be a little snobbish, however. In this area, it seemed to be no big deal to spend money. The Blue Crab was a good, established restaurant, with more than four hundred locations nationwide, but this crowd was used to going to fine dining and privately owned restaurants. Some of them acted as if the Blue Crab was a step down for them.

After working there for the rest of the week, I saw the rest of the crew I used to work with. I had already seen Kareem. Miyah's sister, Stephanie, was also working there as a prep person. It was cool to see her. I had talked to her a few times over the years on the phone. I'd kept in contact with Miyah when I was in Georgia, and Stephanie would jump on the phone and say hello from time to time. Another guy named Leo worked in the prep area as well. We never talked much to each other back in the day. He was cool, but he worked in the kitchen during the day time, and I usually worked in the dining room during the evening. Leo remembered me, though, and said what's up. I ran into Ciara later that weekend. She only worked on the weekend. She had another job and was in school. She was still pretty and nice, just like before. I tried to be slick and ask her if she was still with her boyfriend from back in the day as if I remembered him and thought he was a cool person. Truthfully, I didn't remember what he looked like and was hoping he no longer existed. But she told me they were still together. "It's cool that you're still together," I said. I was lying, and she knew it, too. I knew I had no chance with Ciara, but a brotha had to try.

Leave the Past in the Past

Even though I had been in Georgia for three years and managed to have a girlfriend, not a day passed that I didn't think about Tameka. After all that time, I was still in love with her. Now that I was back home, my thoughts of her intensified. I thought about going to her house the first weekend I was back, but I was afraid of the consequences. I didn't know if she was in a relationship or if she even lived at the same house. I thought about her cursing me out for popping up on her, too. I kept talking myself out of stopping by.

One day, I changed my mind. I was just going to do it. I was nervous about finally seeing her, so I decided I needed to have a drink. I stopped by T.G.I.Friday's and had a stiff drink for a little liquid courage. It was a bad decision. I didn't just have *a* drink, I had several. The drinks were too strong for me, and I had a huge buzz. As I walked back to my car, I saw one of my dear older cousins getting something out of her trunk. She didn't see me. I was ashamed of being slightly drunk, so I tip-toed past her, and I felt guilty about it. I pulled out of the parking lot and drove across the street to the public library to take a nap in their parking lot. I was in no condition to drive.

After I slept off my stupor, I stopped at the gas station to get a Mountain Dew. I needed something to help snap the buzz away. After getting the Mountain Dew, I proceeded to Tameka's house. As I pulled up to her street, I became nervous again. I sat in my car for about ten minutes, contemplating if this was the right thing to do. I finally decided to do it. I crept down her block until I reached her house. There was a car in the driveway, so I knew someone was home. Thoughts crowded my head as I sat in front of her house. *Is this her car or a boyfriend's? What if her boyfriend answers the door? What if it isn't a boyfriend? Is she married now? What if she slaps me or curses me out for coming to her house? What if this isn't even her house anymore? What if she moved?*

Part of me hoped she wasn't there. Unfortunately, I still had quite a lot of liquid courage inside me, clouding my judgment. I took a deep breath, got out of the car, and walked up the stairs to her porch. As I rang her doorbell, I said to myself, "Please don't be home. Please don't be at home."

My wish wasn't granted. I could hear someone approaching the door.

"Who is it?" a woman's voice asked.

I knew immediately it was her. "Um ... This is Carter!" I said, stuttering.

"Who?"

"This is Carter!"

The door opened, and Tameka stood there looking at me through her screen door. She was surprised, with her hand over her mouth in shock.

She was just as beautiful as before. "Hello, Tameka," I said with more certainty.

"Hello, back to you, Carter."

She came outside and gave me a huge hug. Hearing her say my name again melted my heart. She was excited to see me. With tears flowing from her eyes, she invited me into the house and had me sit down at her kitchen table. We talked for about an hour and caught up on everything. She kept saying, "Oh, my god! I can't believe you're here."

I was upset about buzzing so badly. I wasn't myself and couldn't get my words together. I had been waiting three years for this moment, and I was about to mess it up because I was drunk.

I asked her if she was dating anyone. She told me she was, but it wasn't serious, and they hadn't been dating that long. I was happy to hear that. I was back, and there was no way I was going to let her get away again. Unfortunately, she had to pick up her daughter, so I had to leave. I told her I looked forward to talking to her soon.

I left Tameka's house on cloud nine. I hadn't done too bad for being slightly drunk. I made sure I didn't harass her by calling her immediately. I waited a couple of days before I called. When I spoke to her on the phone, she sounded just as excited to talk to me as she had a few days earlier. I kept the conversation brief because I didn't want to seem desperate. I attempted to play it cool. Before I got off the phone with her, she agreed to come to my place to have dinner.

"I'm dying for some king crab legs," she said. "Is tomorrow at six p.m. good?"

"That's perfect," I said and gave her the address, which happened to be my mom's place, but she was out of town for the weekend.

I went to bed early that night because I couldn't wait to get the next day started.

The next morning, to my surprise, Tameka called me bright and early. "Carter, I can't wait to see you later! I'm so excited!"

"I'm just as excited as you are."

"I just called to hear your voice. I have to take my daughter to school." She hung up.

I was back on cloud nine. The three years I'd spent without her was worth it, if it was going to lead to something greater. The day crept by because I was filled with anticipation. I couldn't wait until six o'clock for our date. Finally, as the time drew closer, I went to the Blue Crab and purchased three pounds of crab legs with extra butter and lemons. I also went to the liquor store and bought a bottle of champagne and some strawberries. I stopped at Pier One and bought candles. The last stop was the flower store to get roses. I was going all out for this date. I got back to the house and started setting everything up before Tameka came by. I set the roses in a vase in the middle of the table. I dimmed the lights, and the scented candles lit up the room. I steamed the crab legs to make sure they were piping hot before plating them. I warmed up the butter and set the champagne on ice. It was almost time. I was ready.

It was finally six. I splashed on some cologne and waited near the front door. By six thirty, she wasn't there. I thought I would have to reheat the food, but that would've been no problem. By seven o'clock, she wasn't there yet, but I wasn't pressed. I thought maybe she was running a little late. When she still wasn't there at seven thirty, I started getting a little anxious. I decided to call her, but she didn't pick up the phone. I waited until eight o'clock before calling her again. Still no answer. I knew she wasn't coming. I tried calling her a third time but nothing.

I hung up the phone and threw everything away. I couldn't believe she'd done this to me. All she had to say was that she wasn't interested. I was confused, though, because she had called me that morning, excited about seeing me. *Maybe something happened to her*, I thought. This was destiny. There was no way she'd blown me off.

I jumped into my car to drive by her house and see what was going on. *I hope she wasn't in an accident while trying to come see me. I hope nothing's wrong with her daughter.*

As I drove down her block and got closer to her house, I realized nothing was wrong with her at all. She was standing on her porch, kissing another guy. I crept by, distraught. I was in tears. How could she break my heart again? I felt defeated.

I drove to T.G.I Fridays to have a drink and take away the pain. After getting plastered, I decided to leave Tameka where she needed to be—in the past. It hurt my heart, but I couldn't allow her to let me down again.

BLACK & WHITE

IDECIDED TO NOT CONCENTRATE ON DATING ANYONE BUT FOCUS on working and making money. I started working at the Blue Crab a lot. I enjoyed the new location, but it was a different demographic than I was used to. Including myself and Ciara, there were only four black people working out front in the dining room. There were slightly more in the kitchen: Kareem, Leo, Stephanie, and four guys from Africa. The restaurant was more than ninety percent Caucasian, workers and guests combined.

I first realized how different things were during a customer's birthday at my table. We still had to sing "Happy Birthday," but we now sang the traditional song. I thought it was boring, so when my table had a birthday, I was ready for it. I didn't get any of the other servers to help me. I was going to sing the birthday song all by myself. I had been waiting for this moment. I took my sunglasses out of my pocket and put them on. I started singing my Stevie Wonder rendition of "Happy Birthday" to the customer, bringing some soul to the occasion.

Five seconds into my song, I knew it was a mistake. The dining room froze as my coworkers and every guest stopped what they were doing to look at me. Time stood still as they all stared in disgust. I knew everyone thought I was ghetto and out of place. I looked around as I was singing and stopped mid-song. I took off my sunglasses and said, "Happy birthday" as I walked away. I didn't usually get embarrassed, but this time, I was. I knew, from that moment on, I would only be singing the traditional version of "Happy Birthday."

There was a second time I realized how different this location was. I was in a hurry to get back to the kitchen to get the appetizer that I knew should've been ready by then. I had almost made it to the kitchen when two elderly white ladies stopped me and requested their server. I told them I would be happy to get their server but asked if there was anything I could get for them. We were instructed by our managers to take ownership and try to handle things ourselves when a guest stopped us and asked for something. Most of the time, the guests just wanted a refill on their drinks or more condiments. It was quicker to do it ourselves without making the guests wait, versus trying to find their server and telling the server to go to the table. The elderly ladies said they were waiting on their check, so they could pay and leave. They mentioned that they hadn't seen their server in quite some time. For this, I did need to know the server's identity.

I asked the guest if they remembered who their server was. I wish I hadn't because I was not prepared for the answer.

"She was a short girl, with kinky hair," one of them said.

I thought, *kinky hair?*

"It was a colored girl," the other elderly lady added.

I was beside myself. "Did you say, '*colored* girl'?" I asked. I had never heard the term "colored" outside of old movies. I had to walk away because if I had stayed and encouraged them to continue describing the server, she may have called her something even more demeaning like "nigger," and I would've lost my job.

Another time, I was walking food to a table with three guests: a grandmother, mom, and daughter. They were pleasant people. As I passed out the food, the mom commented on how

154

professional everyone was and said the food looked great. The daughter, who was about eighteen, also commented about how nice it was every time they came. That's when things went south.

The grandmother, who looked to be in her upper eighties, tried to offer a compliment as well. "Yes, our server is a good nigger girl!"

I was stunned. The granddaughter turned red and her mouth dropped in embarrassment. The mom was in disbelief. She immediately apologized. She said her elderly mom was senile and didn't know any better. She asked me to forgive them.

I could tell they were sincere and mortified. The eighteen-year-old was even in tears. This time, instead of walking away, I consoled them. It was my moment to be the bigger person. I don't think the older lady meant anything by it. I knew it wasn't the first time she'd used that word, but I considered that she was in her upper eighties. She probably had grown up hearing that word every day to describe black people. What she'd said wasn't okay, but I decided not to take it personally.

The most shocking example of prejudice I'd seen at this location was not from a white guest but a black family. It was a late Sunday evening, and we had already gotten through our dinner rush. We were down to only a few servers. It was eight p.m. when I was assigned a table with a black family of five. Less than ten percent of our clientele was black. No one would come out and say it, but most of our servers didn't like waiting on black guests because they thought we didn't tip appropriately. That wasn't 100 percent true, but we *did* tend to tip less than fifteen percent. I found it disgusting and tried to teach all my family and friends the proper way to tip.

I went to the table and greeted myself. As I was about to inform them of our specials for the day, the dad stopped me mid-sentence.

"Please don't take this the wrong way," he said, "but we would like another server."

I was shocked and did a self-inventory. Did I do or say

something wrong? Did I come across as being rude? Was my body language off or offensive?

As I stood there interrogating myself, the dad said, "Hey, don't take it personal. You seem to be a good young man. However, we had a long day. I'm a minister, and we've had three services today. I purposely drove past several other Blue Crabs to come to this one. To be honest, we didn't drive all the way out here to be served by a black waiter. I didn't expect to see any black people working here. I wanted to come to an all-white establishment because the service and food would be much better."

I had no words. I had never seen some Uncle Tom shit like that before in my life. What made it worse was that his wife and kids didn't seem shocked or embarrassed. Either, they didn't see anything wrong with his statement, or they were used to his self-loathing behavior.

Once again, I found myself walking away from the table. I went to my manager and informed him of what happened. My manager, Heath, who was white, was pissed off and immediately went to the table. I saw him speaking to the guests and heard the guy ask again for a white server.

"The Blue Crab does not discriminate toward any guest, but the guests are also held to the same standard," Heath explained. "I cannot honor your request. If you aren't happy with who the Blue Crab has decided to hire, you should take your business elsewhere."

To my surprise, the family was appalled. The dad instructed his family to get up and leave. He couldn't believe how they were being treated. "I deserve the right to be waited on by anyone I desire. I am going to report this to your corporate office!"

As he walked past me, he shook his head like I was the one who was wrong. I had to clasp my hands together to prevent both my middle fingers from popping up at him. I thought about the parody character Clayton Bigsby from the *Dave Chappelle Show*. He was a black white supremacist, who didn't realize he was black.

Like Clayton Bigsby, the man must not have realized he was black. I was glad to see his black-white ass get booted from the restaurant.

The next issue I dealt with wasn't a perceived racial issue, but it was a problem for me. Some of the guys liked calling the African workers "The Tribe." I was angered by the nickname. One of the guys teasing them was insecure, and he often made fun of their language. It bothered me because, often, the Africans didn't know they were being made fun of. If someone had called the white guys the Klan, they would've had an issue with it. Most of the guys were good dudes and didn't know any better, and we would later be good friends. They weren't being racist but thought they were being funny. I didn't think it was funny, and I often stated that fact.

CULTURE

I HAD WORKED AT MANY PLACES, BUT SOME OF THE NICEST PEOPLE worked at this location. Everyone took their jobs seriously. A young lady named Burger worked there. I never knew why they called her that, but she was one of the sincerest and nicest people I had ever met. She was nice to everyone she encountered. At first, I thought she was fake. However, it wasn't an act; she was just a wonderful person. Even if she had disgruntled customers, she was always good to them. Everyone complained from time to time but not her. We never heard her even accidentally say something negative about her customers. She'd say that maybe they were having a bad day, and she would pray for them. I liked Burger but not in a romantic way. She was a one-in-a-million type of person, with a big heart.

I went out of my way to help Burger if she needed anything. One day, I was working in a section with her. We were working together as a team and providing excellent service to our guests. Burger and I made great money on the shift. Each of our customers stopped us and thanked us for our service. Some of the customers even asked for the manager and told him how great we were. As we were about to leave, Burger gave me a high five and said, "You rock!"

I laughed because I had never heard that saying before. I told her she rocked as well.

Several of the guys who worked there were gay. It didn't bother me, but it was different. I had never *knowingly* worked with or interacted with gay men before. It didn't take me long to realize they were just as cool as anyone else. I didn't catch on until I realized the amount of attention one of the guys received from our female customers. The Blue Crab was his second job. His main job was as a personal trainer, so he was in great shape. A lot of the female customers hit on him, and some were beautiful, but he paid them no attention. None of our female coworkers tried to date him. I was confused. I thought maybe he was married and not interested. When his boyfriend came to the restaurant, I finally got it.

A few months after I had started working there, they hired another gay server named Matt. He was a good server, but he was sarcastic and slightly rude. Either his customers loved him or hated him. The same went for the crew, but I was indifferent. Matt didn't bother me. Plus, his sister was hot, and I had a small crush on her, so it made working with Matt a little easier.

One day, I came into the kitchen to drop off my dirty dishes at the dish ring. There were only a few of us in the kitchen. As I put up the dishes, someone grabbed my butt and walked off quickly. It wasn't a slight graze or accidental hit. It was a full hand grab and squeeze. At first, I didn't think anything of it. A lot of the girls played around. They'd slap each other's butts or slap the butts of one of the gay guys. A few of the girls had hit me on the butt before when they were playing around. I didn't see which girl did it because a wall separated the dish area from the rest of the kitchen. After I put up my dishes and came around the corner, I saw there was only one server in the kitchen, Matt. I was confused.

He looked at me and smiled.

I asked him, "Who was just in the kitchen?"

"Two people just walked out."

I was more confused. I knew he hadn't grabbed my butt. I started to ask him, but all I could say was, "Nah."

"Nah, what?" he asked.

"Never mind."

He walked in my direction. "You look confused. Yes, it was me who grabbed your butt!" he confessed with a cocky smirk. He tried to walk past me.

I was beside myself and reacted faster than I thought I ever could. In an instant, I had pushed Matt against the wall with a fist full of his collar in both hands, lifting him off the ground. I looked him straight in the eyes and said, "If you ever put you muthafuckin' hands on me again, I will fuck you up!"

Matt was startled and apologized immediately.

I let him go, but I was still fuming. That was the second time I had spoken to someone that way on the job. The first time, I felt bad for overreacting, but this time, I had no regrets. He was lucky I didn't start punching him first. Luckily, no one else was around. I would've gotten fired.

Another one of my male coworkers was one of the most insecure people I had ever met. He was extremely skinny, almost anorexic. Due to his appearance, he felt he needed to be defensive. He talked badly about people until sometimes, they were in tears. I laughed when he tried to talk about me. I felt sorry for him. Unfortunately, I could also hurt people's feelings with my words. I was careful not to always say what was on my mind. He didn't want me to express my feelings toward him. I didn't understand why the managers let him get away with his verbal assaults and outbursts. Maybe it was because he was good at what he did and could work multiple positions in the kitchen. That didn't make it okay for him to be so nasty.

During one shift, the managers bought pizza for the entire crew. Unfortunately, the only place where we could eat was in the back of the kitchen. There were about fifteen boxes of pizza. At the end of the night, the pizza boxes were everywhere, and it was his job to clean up the back of the kitchen. He was furious because no one bothered to throw any of the boxes away. He launched a verbal assault on the entire crew as he tossed boxes everywhere. He was upset with me because, in the middle of his tantrum, I laughed. He yelled at me for laughing at him. He thought it was unfair that we didn't have to help clean. If he had simply asked for help, I would've. However, I didn't respond well to people's foolishness. I had to get away from him before I cursed him out.

• • •

One evening, I was working in the smoking section with Burger. We were slammed and should have had more help. Burger and I were doing our best, but we couldn't keep up. We had too many tables and couldn't handle it. It was Saturday and, typically, we wouldn't be too busy for lunch. But this Saturday was crazy busy from the start. A few hours into the shift, we got more servers to relieve some of the craziness. However, the damage was done. We were in the weeds.

Burger had about seven tables going. I also had seven tables, but three of them were cashed out and waiting. I noticed a guest at one of Burger's tables was raising her voice at her. Burger remained calm as she apologized to the rude lady and her daughter for the delay with the food. The lady told Burger to walk away and get the manager. Lexi, the manager, was a little busy. She was in the back of the kitchen, prepping food. She told Burger she would be at the table in a few minutes. Lexi was afraid of guest confrontation and tried her best to stay in the kitchen.

Burger had to go back to the dining room to service the rest of her guests. She went to the table and told the rude lady she had talked to the manager, and she would be right over. I asked Burger if she was okay and she said she was.

"The guests are frustrated, and they should be. It's not their fault we're understaffed," she explained with her usual compassion.

After ten minutes, as Burger and I worked as fast as we

could, the rude guest yelled for Burger from across the smoking section. When Burger came back to the table, she yelled at her because the manager still hadn't come to the table. I could tell, for the first time, the guest's behavior was getting to Burger. She, once again, apologized. Midway through her apology, the guest picked up her orange soda and threw it into Burger's face. "Now, bitch, go and get your manager!" she screamed.

Burger turned red and started crying as she ran away from the table. I went after her to console her. I may have been arrested if I had stopped at the table first. People tended to forget that just because we were serving them, we were still people. They didn't have the right to disrespect us or put their hands on us. Had she thrown the soda in my face, I would've reacted before thinking, and it would've been bad.

Burger made it to the kitchen, and she was visibly upset, crying uncontrollably. I had never seen her upset, and it hurt me. Lexi came running over to us to see what happened. Everyone told her about how the guest had thrown soda in Burger's face. We all wanted Lexi to kick them out.

As we consoled Burger, we were informed that her rude customer's food was ready. Lexi immediately grabbed the food and went out into the dining room and served the guest. I overheard her talking to the woman, and she lied on Burger.

"She was so rude!"

"I'm very sorry about that," Lexi said. "Did you throw a soda on her?"

"Yes, I threw it, but it was out of frustration," she admitted. "I have never had poor service here before. I was just a little upset."

"I'm very sorry, ma'am. It will never happen again."

I was appalled. Heath would've kicked them out with the quickness.

When Lexi came back into the kitchen, everyone confronted her for not kicking the customers out. She decided to justify their behavior and even had the audacity to counsel Burger on her lack of service. I was blown away.

Without being asked, I decided to take over Burger's table. I rudely told the guests I would be taking over their service for the remainder of their visit. I got them a refill for their sodas and slammed it down on the table. I looked at the guest who had thrown her soda at Burger, daring her with my eyes as if to say, "Bitch, I wish you would think about throwing that soda in my face!"

She got the point. She and her daughter asked for takeout boxes, and they left immediately.

That was the first time since working with Veronica in the South I thought about being a manager. At first, I was intimidated by the new location, but after seeing the poor job Lexi was doing as a manager, I knew I could do better.

I couldn't stand Lexi. She was afraid to talk to guests and would avoid confrontation by staying in the kitchen. She must've been great at paperwork or invoicing because she was horrible at anything that required verbal skill. She was good at abusing her authority, however. There were times when I had something to do and needed to get off work early. I would tell Lexi at the beginning of our shift, and she'd say she couldn't make any promises, but she would try. When it started to slow down, Lexi would cut everyone else first and find a way to keep me for as long as possible.

On the days I wanted to make more money and stay longer, Lexi would find a way to cut me first. I didn't know what this lady's problem was with me. I eventually got smart about it and made it into a game. I switched it up on her. On the days I wanted to leave early, I begged Lexi to let me stay because I needed to make money. She'd promise to try to keep me, but she always made me go home first. When I needed to make money, I told Lexi I needed to go, and I would be the last to go home. I laughed about it. I had planned to report her to Sal, but I didn't think he'd care. Sal and I never hit it off, so instead of complaining about it, I continued to play my game, and Lexi never realized what I was doing. I told some of the other servers about my tactics, and they did the same. We had a blast every time one of us used reverse psychology on her.

Some of the servers took advantage of her. They knew she wasn't going to talk to customers unless it was the last resort. Lexi would rather buy the food for the guests instead of talking to them. Some of the servers would tell Lexi the guests were irate and wanted to talk to the manager. Instead of going to the table, Lexi would ask the server what happened. They'd say something about the guests not liking the food, and Lexi would tell the server to let the guests know their food was on the house. She didn't realize the servers were lying to her. There was no disgruntled guest. They'd wait until someone had paid with cash and left and tell Lexi the story. She bought it every time. Meanwhile, the server pocketed the cash. They knew not to try that when Sal or Heath was there. Heath was always in the dining room. It would've been impossible to get over on him.

Heath

HEATH WAS A GOOD MANAGER. HE WAS FAIR, CONSISTENT, AND got along with everyone. He told me I should consider going into management. He said the salary was nice, but the quarterly bonuses were what kept him. They allowed him to pay his mortgage for up to three months at a time. I thought that was cool, even though managing was just a thought for me.

Heath worked at the Blue Crab at a time when anyone who worked there could stay and drink after work, and he was a heavy drinker. I can't remember a day when Heath got off work and didn't have a drink. He was always calm and cool, except when he had been drinking. He'd start stuttering and could barely stand up. I don't know how he was getting home from work. Sal should've put a stop to it, but he was rarely at the restaurant past two p.m. He'd take off and go golfing somewhere, so he never knew much about Heath's problem.

Heath was a ladies' man. Many of the female servers and guests loved him, and he took advantage of that fact. He was usually sleeping with at least two different workers at the same time. They all knew it, too, but they didn't mind.

Sometimes, when the dinner crew got off late, to reward the kitchen for a great day or cleaning up well, Heath would give them drinks at the bar. After a few rounds, he'd say it was time to go. Many of the crew members would go next door to the twenty-four-hour breakfast restaurant and grab something to eat. They'd invite Heath, but he always said he had to get home. At first, the crew thought nothing of it. However, one night, when they were done eating at the restaurant next door, they came back to the Blue Crab to get their cars from the parking lot and noticed Heath's car was parked on the other side of the building, opposite from where he was originally parked. The crew members thought maybe Heath had forgotten something, but after a few minutes had passed and he didn't come outside, they thought something may be wrong. They decided to walk toward the building where the windows were. All the lights were off in the restaurant, and they were getting worried. Someone even suggested calling the police. They thought maybe Heath was getting robbed.

Someone else peered into the window and said, "Don't call the police!" He told the others to come look.

At first glance, no one saw anything. Then they saw it! Heath was inside, but he wasn't alone. He was sitting at a booth with a woman with long blonde hair. They couldn't tell who she was. Everyone was drunk and excited, so they decided to watch and see what was going on. Heath and the woman were talking, and it led to kissing. Then the woman disappeared. When Heath relaxed his head on the back of the booth, they realized she was underneath, pleasuring him. After a few minutes, she came back up and they could finally see her. She was one of our servers!

They watched in awe as Heath bent her over the table and started having sex with her. They enjoyed the show for a while before going back to their cars, laughing. The server was one of the girls who had stayed to have drinks that night, but she had declined to go eat with the crew, also claiming she had to go.

Heath's sexual escapades became a weekly occurrence. I was surprised he was never caught.

SAL

I NEVER SAW EYE TO EYE WITH SAL. HE WAS A GREAT MANAGER, and I loved when he was in the restaurant. We could always tell when he was there just by walking in. Everyone worked harder. The managers were fairer and more consistent, and the crew did things without being asked. Sal ensured the restaurant stayed clean. He had no tolerance for a dirty dining room. When he was working, we'd see him walking around with a pot of coffee, refilling the guests' cups. We never saw him bus a table. He stayed smooth and clean, and he'd bite our heads off if our section was dirty. I made sure I kept my section clean. I didn't want any problems.

However, while working a Saturday shift, we were severely understaffed. I had too many tables, and I was having a hard time keeping up. I was running eleven tables with no assistance. It gave me flashbacks of when I had walked out in Georgia, but I wasn't going to walk out this time. No one complained, but I knew they weren't getting the best service.

Sal didn't work that morning and had come in for the dinner shift. As he walked through the dining room, he noticed my section was a wreck. As soon as he saw me, he pulled me to the side. "Carter, get your section together immediately!"

"Sal, it's extremely busy, and I need some help!"

Sal didn't want to hear any excuses. "You better get your section together right now. You won't get another table until it's spotless!"

I didn't want any more tables, so I was sure not to clean up too quickly, fearing I would be back in the weeds.

After Sal set me straight, he went into the kitchen, and it was in equally bad shape. Lexi was in the back, bouncing from the cook line and prep. She was in her element, not running the restaurant. Since she was busy, Sal decided to place himself squarely into the kitchen to get some order. A lot of orders were ready, but the expo was having a hard time getting the servers to run them. Sal started by getting the food run to the dining room. One of mine was the first ready to go.

"Carter, run this food to your table," he ordered.

"Okay, but I need a second."

He looked me straight in the eyes. "You need to get this food out of this kitchen *right now*. I want it out while it's hot and ready to go."

I dropped what I was doing and walked my food out. As soon as I came back into the kitchen, he told me I had another tray of food ready to go out.

"Can I please just run these drinks out to my table first?"

"Hurry up, but come right back to get this food."

I returned to the kitchen a few minutes later to grab my food. As I was walking out with the tray, I heard Sal call my name and order someone else to run my next tray. Over the next ten minutes, more and more orders for my tables came up. After Sal had servers walk four more trays out, he said, "Holy shit! How many tables do you have?"

"That's what I've been trying to tell you. I have too many tables. I have eleven!"

He was visibly pissed that I had that many tables, not at me but the manager for allowing the host to sit me that way. If he just would've taken the time to listen to me in the first place, he would've known.

That wasn't the first or last time Sal and I had a misunderstanding. The Blue Crab wanted to promote some of its employees into more leadership roles. After talking it over with his management team, Sal decided four other team members and I would be shift leaders. I was excited about the opportunity. He scheduled a meeting for the five of us. Unfortunately, I was doubled scheduled. The meeting was scheduled at eleven a.m., but I was already scheduled to set up the kitchen at nine a.m. I made it to the meeting ten minutes late because I was finishing up in the kitchen. When I came and sat down, I could tell Sal was pissed at me. He never acknowledged me during the meeting, like I wasn't even there.

The weeks following the meeting, I noticed the other people who were at the meeting started getting scheduled for leadership shifts. Of course, I was never given a shift or even mentioned for one. I was a little annoyed about it, but I let it go. It wasn't until I had a conversation with Sal that I got heated about it again. We were working, and it was steady. One of the shift leaders had called off for their serving shift. It wasn't a big deal, but we had two new servers working, and they needed to shadow someone. They put one server with a shift leader but didn't have anyone for the second new server to follow. Sal mentioned to the shift leader that he may have to train two servers at the same time. The shift leader pushed back, stating it was too busy to train one server, let alone two. Sal conceded and apologized to the other new server and told her she could go home and finish training the next day.

"I can train her, Sal," I volunteered.

He looked at me and then looked back at the new server. "I'll see you tomorrow," he said to her.

I was dumbfounded. He would rather send her home than let me train her! I started thinking this was no longer the place for me.

At the end of the shift, Sal and the shift leader were in the office. I stopped by and asked Sal if I could speak to him.

He said, "Sure, what's up?"

"Why don't you want me training anyone?"

Sal looked at me like I had insulted him. "How dare you ask me that question, when you didn't even show up for the shift leader meeting!"

"I *was* at the meeting. You probably didn't remember because you never acknowledged me."

"Dude, what do you mean? You weren't at the meeting!" He looked at the shift leader for confirmation. The shift leader stated that I was at the meeting. Sal looked embarrassed and tried to cover it up with more cockiness. "Why didn't you sign the roster for the attendees like everyone else did? I had to turn in the sign-in sheet to my boss, and your name was never on it."

"I don't recall signing in."

"Everyone signed in at the beginning of the meeting."

"I was a little late to the meeting," I started to explain.

Sal cut me off. "Okay, you were late to a leadership meeting," he retorted.

"I was the only one double scheduled, and I was setting up the kitchen when the meeting started."

Sal had nothing else to say. He realized his disdain for me was ridiculous. He apologized and said he would look into getting me scheduled for some of the shift leader shifts. Sal and I got along better after that. We didn't have a great relationship, but it was, indeed, better.

You Knock Me Off My Feet

We had a server name Alfred, who was a passionate employee. He was a professional. He didn't come to work to hang out with anyone; he came to do his job. His table presence was amazing, and he conducted himself like a fine-dining server. He had a professional greeting, and he was articulate when describing the menu. Guests loved him, but his team didn't always care for him.

He was a large guy and a little clumsy. He bumped into people, and he would almost run us over like he didn't see us as he tried to walk straight through us. The employees complained about it constantly. Plenty of times, he had knocked someone's tray out of their hand because he wasn't looking where he was going. He'd even done it to me on several occasions.

It was worse when dropping dishes off at the dish area. Several times, I would be breaking my tray of dishes down, and when I stepped back, Alfred was standing right there. He never announced his presence, so I'd walk into him and almost fall off balance, like bouncing off a big, rubbery wall. As it happened repeatedly, I began to get frustrated. We told the managers about it, but they said they didn't think Alfred was doing it on purpose; he was just a big guy. At first, I let it go, but after continuous collisions, I couldn't any longer. I confronted Alfred. Other people had confronted him as well, and he was defensive, but other people weren't my concern. I decided to have a talk with him and, of course, he became defensive with me, too.

I wasn't sure if he was doing it on purpose or not, but I was sick of him running into me, making me drop things. Since the managers wouldn't handle it, I decided to. I had to be careful because I didn't want to get fired. I made sure I ran into him. Since I was much smaller than him, I knew merely bumping into him would be a loss for me, so I hit him with a tray upon impact, making it seem like an accident. I planned to keep doing it until he got the point. It only took two times for him to get it.

The first time, I waited until the kitchen was busy, with a lot of servers. He always carried his tray high. I had a tray sitting on the counter as I watched him approach, bumping into everyone along the way. I timed it to where I would be turning in his direction as he tried to make it past me. We were so busy that no one noticed me. I turned toward him with a lot of force and perfectly hit his extended elbow with my tray. His tray went flying, along with everything on it. He bent over in pain. I immediately went to check on him like I was concerned. I didn't want to injure him, but I did want him to feel a little pain. I heard other servers, whom he'd run over previously, snickering in the background. I even heard someone say, "That's what his big ass gets." I laughed on the inside, careful not to let it show.

I thought he would've gotten the point, but Alfred continued bumping into me and others. The next time I got him, I came into the dish area as he was putting up his dishes. I stood right behind him as he normally did with other people. I held my tray with both hands as I waited for him to turn around. As soon as he turned around, I moved a couple of steps toward him and hit him in the head with the tray. Alfred went down to one knee. Instantly, I put my tray down and went into acting mode. He had a big whelp on his head. I almost felt bad, but I stopped those thoughts immediately. Countless times, Alfred had knocked people down or hit them on the head. I stood there, looking at him like Muhammad Ali towering Sonny Liston. I knew I had made my point.

Alfred went home for the day after complaining about his head throbbing. I hoped he didn't have a concussion. A few servers asked me if I had done it on purpose. I told them, "Of course not!" They smiled at me because they knew I had planned it. After that, no one ever had an issue with Alfred again.

Pepé Le Pew

S OME OF THE EMPLOYEES' POOR HYGIENE WAS A KNOWN PROBLEM at work. I'd come into work and walk past some of the employees and almost pass out due to the smell. Some people thought if they just put on cologne or body lotion, it would mask their musty smell. Instead, it served as an enhancer. Funk and cologne is a horrible mixture. Quite a few of the employees were funky.

One guy, however, took the cake. I called him Pepé Le Pew, after the skunk cartoon character. He was the funk champion! I never encountered someone on his level of funk. If shit had a cologne, he was wearing it. Even worse, he wanted to touch us all the time and be in our personal space, and his hands felt gritty like something was on them. Even worse, he was a host, the first and last person the guests encountered when entering and leaving the restaurant. The host could make or break the entire experience. I couldn't believe they put him up front. Everyone knew he smelled horrible, including the managers. Some of the guests complained about him, but the managers never addressed it. I wasn't sure if his poor hygiene practices were because of his religion or what, but I had never heard of a religion that required you to rub shit all over your body.

Comedian and actor Jaime Foxx once spoke about an encounter he'd had with someone who smelled bad. He had gone out of the country and was standing next to a foreign guy. The guy smelled awful but was confused by Jamie's smell. As Jamie started sniffing, he looked at the guy and asked, "What is that smell?"

Confused, the foreign guy looked at Jamie and asked, "Yes, what is that smell?" He thought Jamie's lotion and soap were smelly.

Jamie Foxx farted, and the guy instantly became happy. "Oh my God, what is that wonderful fragrance?" he said.

The host reminded me of Jamie's story. His smell was so bad that we could follow his scent to find him. I stayed as far away from him as possible, afraid his stench could enter my clothes. If he was at one end of the kitchen, I walked the other way to get out of the kitchen and avoid walking past. I'd never encountered someone who could make my stomach hurt and eyes water every time I came within ten feet of them. A single person should not smell that bad!

I couldn't take it anymore; I had to go to Sal. Sal was in the office with another manager when I confronted him about the smelly guy. I was hesitant to say anything to Sal since we were getting along fairly well; however, no one in the restaurant wanted to talk about the shitty elephant in the room. Everyone talked about him in small circles but didn't want to address it. When I expressed my concerns to Sal and Lexi, they both acknowledged his foul odor. Of course, Lexi wasn't going to do anything, but Sal surely would handle it. Sal told me it was a delicate matter, and they didn't want to offend him. "Since you're the shift leader, you should handle it," he suggested.

I was surprised the general manager didn't want to handle the situation. It was no sweat for me, though. I was young and cocky. Confrontation didn't bother me. I immediately went and found Pepé Le Pew. I pulled him to the side and started talking to him. I was beating around the bush because it was a little difficult to tell someone they smelled like shit. Pepé noticed I was stalling. He told me to say whatever was on my mind.

I just came out with it and told him, "People are complaining about your smell."

He seemed to have no idea he was funky, and he was offended. "No one else has complained about it, so who are you to confront me about it?"

"Everyone, including the guests, is complaining about it," I explained.

He became irate. "If it's a problem, management will have to talk to me!"

"The managers have a problem with your smell as well, but they didn't want to hurt your feelings."

He stormed off, cursing, and he was hostile for the remainder of his shift.

Although he remained smelly, he never spoke to me again and avoided me whenever possible. I didn't mind. I was grateful and so were my nose hairs.

WASTED WEDNESDAYS

I STARTED HANGING OUT WITH SOME OF THE OTHER WORKERS, mainly the kitchen staff. It was unusual to have such good rapport with the kitchen staff because I worked in the front of the house. Only three servers hung out with the kitchen crew. I was probably allowed to hang with them because I was familiar with two of the kitchen workers, Leo and Stephanie. We would all go out on Wednesdays and called it "Wasted Wednesday." We hardly ever missed a Wasted Wednesday. Although I was good friends with Stephanie's sister, Miyah, I had developed a solid friendship with Stephanie. She was hilarious and always laughing. Leo and the other guys were fun as well. The kitchen guys made up hilarious names for the other employees.

One of the funniest names was F-150. I'd heard them say it while we were at work, but I never knew the meaning until I started going out to Wasted Wednesdays with them. I asked them why they called one of the female workers F-150, and they told me to look outside. A Ford F-150 pickup truck was parked out front. I didn't get it. Leo told me to think about the woman and look at the truck. I still didn't get it.

"It's a flatbed truck," I said.

They all laughed. "Now, do you get it?"

I still didn't understand, until Leo said, "Look at it again. The truck is big in the front and flat in the back."

I almost died from laughter because it described her perfectly. She had giant breasts but no butt.

Another funny name they'd given someone was OFYA. Before I asked them what it stood for, I tried to figure it out, but I couldn't. The guys would never come out and tell me. They always made me crack the code. They told me to describe the woman. She was a little older than us, but she was in great shape. She was an okay server and a little whiny.

They said, "What does everyone notice about her?"

"We all notice her behind," I replied. She had a nice figure and an even better behind.

Once again, they laughed and said I had figured it out. Leo said, "OFYA stands for old face, young ass."

I broke into uncontrollable laughter again because she, indeed, had an old face and a great ass. She could've been called OFGA for *great* ass. Younger male customers would see her walk by and try to get her attention as they stared at her backside. As soon as she turned around, though, they changed their mind. She wasn't an ugly woman, but she was older than most guys thought when they saw her from behind.

There were many more nicknames but one I wasn't too keen on. They had a nickname for me. I was obsessed with one of the young ladies who worked there. She was gorgeous, with a wonderful body and an equally wonderful personality. Her name was Mandy. I was a fan of Mandy, and everyone knew it. I tried everything to be on her good side. I wanted to go out with her, and I wasn't cool about it, either. Unfortunately, she wasn't interested in me. I still tried but was always unsuccessful.

I got her phone number from the employee roster and called her. She was polite when I called, but she told me she wasn't interested. I took her kindness for an invitation, however. I thought because she was so nice to me, she must've liked me a little. After a few weeks, I decided to call her again. This time, she wasn't so nice. She seemed agitated. I could hear a guy in the background, yelling for her to give him the phone so he could talk to me. She told me never to call her again and hung up.

When Mandy saw me at work, she was still pleasant. I figured her boyfriend was an asshole, and she didn't know how to break it off with him. She always said hello to me and gave me a hug. *I know she likes me!* I thought.

I had flowers delivered anonymously to the restaurant to surprise her. I saw her when she got the flowers, and she was, indeed, surprised. Her green eyes brightened as the delivery person gave her the bouquet. I watched as she opened the card I had written, and she burst into tears. Finally, she understood how much I liked her.

I went back to serving my tables, but I didn't see Mandy any longer. I asked one of her work friends if they had seen her.

"She's in the office with the managers."

I was worried about her. Twenty minutes later, I saw a guy go into the back with the managers as well. He seemed upset about something. I figured, he must've been a disgruntled guest, but I had never seen a guest go into our manager's office.

I didn't know what was going on until I heard some of the girls talking. They said the guy was Mandy's boyfriend, and they overheard him yelling at the managers. A few minutes later, Mandy and her boyfriend walked out of the building together. She didn't have the flowers I'd sent her.

One of the managers asked to sit down and talk to me. I hoped nothing bad had happened to Mandy. They all knew I liked her, and I would've been crushed if I found out her boyfriend was doing something bad to her.

The manager said, "Look, dude, you have to stop this obsession with Mandy immediately!"

Luckily, this manager was one of the cool ones. She was new to the restaurant, and I knew one of her sisters and her brother.

"Mandy was upset about you sending her flowers, so she called her boyfriend to complain about you. She had no idea he would come up here, but he did. Fortunately, I was up front when he walked in because he was only looking for Mandy so he could come after you. I was able to get him to calm down and told him he needs to let the Blue Crab handle this. He didn't want to listen, but I assured him I would handle the situation and it would never happen again."

I hung my head in shame.

"Carter, what you're doing is borderline harassment."

I was embarrassed. I didn't think it was that bad, but apparently, it was.

"I won't report this to Sal, but if you continue with this behavior, I *will* report you and fire you myself."

"I understand," I said. "Thank you for saving my job."

The next day, when I came to work, Mandy was in the lobby waiting for me. I thought she was going to give me paperwork from the police station, instructing me to stay away from her. But she asked to sit down and talk to me in a kind but firm tone.

"Carter, you seem like a great guy, but I have a boyfriend, and I'm happy with him. You make me feel uncomfortable when we work together."

I felt terrible. "I'm sorry, Mandy. You won't have to worry about me ever again," I promised. I meant it, and I think she knew it. She thanked me and gave me a hug.

I didn't bother her anymore, but it was too late; the entire crew knew I was crazy about her. The Wasted Wednesdays crew had nicknamed me "Mr. Mandy." That name stuck with me for a year. I tried to play it cool, but I was embarrassed every time someone said it.

SHADY

Although we worked with a lot of women, after the embarrassment of becoming Mr. Mandy, I did my best to avoid going out with anyone I worked with. I stayed on track for about a year. That changed, however, when they hired a new server, Lisa. I never went after Lisa, but she came after me. She was flirtatious, and she flirted with almost every male guest that came into the restaurant. She was money hungry as well. If a guy had money, she was all over him. She was one of the type of girls who got dressed up in tight, revealing clothes to go to NBA games, trying to capture the attention of men with money. Clearly, when she flirted with me, it wasn't for the money. I had none.

Lisa was a freak. Daily, I caught her at the other end of the kitchen, sticking her tongue out at me in a sexual manner. I thought she was a big tease. Whenever we had a break at work, she asked me to go to the store with her. She'd drive with her left hand on the steering wheel and her right hand in my pants. It happened at least once a week. I constantly asked her to come over my place, but she never would. I got sick and tired of her teasing me, so I started to ignore her. After a few weeks, she decided to come over my house. We had fun and finally sealed the deal.

"I'm sorry for not coming over before. I didn't come because I'm married," she explained.

I was floored! Her husband was an older, retired man. He was always at home and constantly checking up on her. I couldn't believe she was that promiscuous as a married woman. I had told myself I would never mess with a married woman. Although I felt bad, I didn't let it bother me too much because I hadn't known. She didn't care at all. I had a feeling I wasn't the first person she'd cheated on her husband with, and I wouldn't be the last.

The next day, I went to work and was relieved she wasn't there. I was still slightly bothered by her revelation but decided to let it go. Some hours later, the host told me a table had requested me as their server. I thought nothing of it because tables often requested me. The host told me my table had requested the smoking section. That wasn't my section, but I had no problem going to pick up the table.

I was shocked when I got there. Lisa had requested me, and she wasn't alone. She was with an older guy I was hoping was her dad. They were sitting on the same side of the booth, and they were holding hands. Before I could react, she introduced us.

"Hey, Carter! It's my husband's birthday, and he wanted to eat here."

He shook my hand. "Nice to meet you," he said.

He seemed to be a nice guy. As we chatted, Lisa did that tongue thing at me behind his back. I was instantly turned off, disgusted that she was such a horrible person. Every time I came back to the table, she made a sexual gesture toward me behind his back. She thought it was cute and turning me on, which couldn't have been further from the truth. I knew, at that moment, I would never sleep or flirt with her again.

Maybe It's You

THE LONGER I WORKED AT THE BLUE CRAB AND HUNG OUT WITH the employees, the more I complained about the job, just like they did. I complained about everything, from management, fellow team members, and the guests. When I had first arrived at that location, I made more money than I had ever made at any Blue Crab. The tips were amazing. However, after being there more than a year, I started to see the tips go down. And some of the customers were ridiculous. They always wanted everything to be perfect, and they ran us to death. I hated when I asked the customers if they needed anything else and after saying no, they asked for something when I came back. I talked to some of the other servers about it, and many of them said the same thing.

The tips started getting so bad that I decided to pick up a second job. I changed my schedule at the Blue Crab to Saturday and Sunday only. I worked my other job at a temp service Monday through Friday, and I worked double shifts at the Blue Crab on the weekend. I wanted to get hired full-time at my temp job. I was working for a large company, and the pay was generous if hired directly. Unfortunately, I was hired through the temp company and was only making nine dollars an hour. I would make almost double if I could get a permanent hire, so I stuck around. It was rough working seven days a week, but I didn't want to let the Blue Crab go until I was sure I could get the job with the other company. I was making more money working doubles on Saturdays and Sundays at the Blue Crab than I was by working full-time for the temp company.

After six months, I decided to let the temp service go and go back to working full-time with the Blue Crab until I found something else better suited for me. It was a big relief to go back to working forty hours instead of doubles on the weekend, but nothing had changed. The managers, crew, and customers were still horrible. I eventually worked lunch shifts only, and my goal was to get twenty tables per shift. I figured if each table gave me at least three dollars, I would make sixty dollars for the day. That goal kept me going until I could find another job. I wasn't concerned about giving great service any longer. I just wanted to turn and burn my tables, get them in and get them out.

Some other servers were making better money than I was, and I was getting pissed. I knew some of them were slow, and they couldn't handle as many tables as I could. For a moment, I even thought it was because I was black. My complaints to other servers grew worse. I was always in the kitchen, speaking ill of my customers. I couldn't stand them or the Blue Crab anymore.

One of the guys got tired of hearing me complain. He had only been working there for a month, and we rarely conversed. In the middle of one of my rants, he stopped me and said, "Maybe you should just quit!"

I was taken aback by his comment. "What?" I asked aggressively.

He wouldn't let up. "I haven't been working here that long, but in the short time I've been here, I've listened to you complain about the customers every day."

"Well, the customers here suck!"

"Have you ever thought about the fact that it could be *you*?"

Now, I was really pissed.

"I make really good money and so do others. If you would stop bitching about the customers and just take care of them, maybe you would make better money, too."

"When I want your opinion, I'll ask for it," I spat.

I was angry about our conversation for the rest of the shift. Even when I got off and went home, I was still pissed. But the more I thought about it, I realized he was right. I wasn't as good as I used to be as a server. I spent way too much time complaining instead of doing the work. This dude, whom I didn't even know, had done the best thing for me by saying what I needed to hear.

I thought about it the entire night. I couldn't wait to get back to work. I decided, from that point on, I would be the best server any customer could get at any restaurant. I decided to study the menu more and be an exceptional server. I never thanked the guy for saying that to me, and I didn't make a big announcement. I just changed.

I saw immediate benefits from my behavioral change and outlook toward the customers. I stopped trying to get as many tables as possible and focused on giving personalized service. I remembered guests by name and memorized their favorite meals. I catered to my guests' every need. I found time to crack their crab legs for them, and I put their crab bibs on them. I even walked their bags out to their cars. I engrossed myself into being the best experience maker for my customers. If it was raining outside, I grabbed the Blue Crab umbrella and walked the guests to their cars. It became contagious. I didn't care if it wasn't my table, I helped any guest. I even started buying desserts for my tables, making a point to buy at least one dessert for a table every shift I worked. Since we received fifty percent off our food, it only cost me about three dollars per shift. The payback was enormous. I got bigger tips and more requests.

I also stopped taking things personally. I embraced my guests and never let anything bother me. Several guests would come into the restaurant already in a foul mood. Instead of getting upset with them, I killed them with kindness. But kindness could only go so far, I also had to deliver great service. I took it as a challenge when I received a customer with an attitude. I never let them see me sweat. I also learned to agree with the customer, even if I knew they were wrong.

Although I didn't make an announcement, everyone noticed the change in my attitude. But the change was, most importantly, reflected in the amount of tips I brought home each day. I had doubled the tips I was previously making. On rare occasions, it was tripled. Several servers commented about how great it was to work with me. My managers took notice as well. They knew if one of my tables asked for a manager, it was to give a compliment. I handled every situation at the table myself, so a manager didn't have to get involved.

Because of the attitude change, some of my managers and fellow team members suggested I think about going into management. At first, I brushed it off because I wasn't sure if I wanted to stay in the restaurant industry. Some customers were trying to get me to work for their companies, and I was also trying to become a sheriff. Unfortunately, none of those ventures were working out for me, so I finally decided to look into management at the Blue Crab.

I inquired with Sal about the position, but he blew me off. His managers had even suggested he give me a chance, but he still showed no interest. He told me I had no kitchen experience, and they were looking at candidates who were well rounded. So, I started coming in on my own time and learning how to work in different positions, and I didn't ask to be clocked in. A few of my buddies worked in the kitchen, so they trained me on different positions.

Sal came in and saw me working in the kitchen. "What's going on, Carter?" he asked.

"Don't worry, Sal. I'm not affecting your labor hours. I'm just working to get some kitchen experience."

"It's great that you're trying to learn, but you can't work off the clock because it's a labor law violation, and I can get into trouble for it."

I understood. I was upset because it stopped my training, but it didn't deter me. I continued to train in the kitchen on my own time, but I made sure Sal wasn't in the building when I did so.

I continued to try to impress Sal, but it was to no avail. Since he showed no interest, I decided to contact his supervisor, our area director, Chris. I told Chris I was interested in going into management, but I was unsure of the proper course to take. Chris usually came into the restaurant once a week, so he already knew I was a good server. "Do you have any experience working in the kitchen?" he asked.

"No, I've never worked in the kitchen, but I have no problem learning."

"I can't promise you anything, but I'll talk to Sal about it first and get back with you."

I told myself to forget about it. I didn't think Sal would have anything positive to say about me.

The next day, I came into work, and Sal was waiting to speak to me. He had me come to the manager's office. He expressed that he was upset with me for going over his head to talk to his boss.

I calmly told him, "I don't believe you're taking me seriously. I have done everything possible to become a model employee, and I want to move to the next level. Since you didn't take me seriously, I moved on to the person who could make it happen for me."

Surprisingly, Sal wasn't upset. "I really didn't think you were serious," he said. "I will do what I can to help you if you are, indeed, serious."

I thought he was blowing smoke up my behind, but a couple of weeks later, Chris gave me a call. He told me I would have to take a drug test, and he asked if I would pass. I was offended, and I think Chris realized that. He immediately advised me if I failed the required drug test, not only would I not be eligible for management, but he would have to terminate me. I told him the drug test would be no problem.

A few days later, someone from the Blue Crab's corporate office called me and scheduled the test, with a five-hour window to complete it. They gave me a list of nearby facilities to get it done, and I went immediately. I even called Chris when I was done. He told me once the results came in, I would have to take a written exam. The next day, the results came in and, to no surprise, I had passed. Chris called and told me he would be in the restaurant the following week to give me the written exam.

I was nervous when it was time to take the exam. I couldn't concentrate, and it was timed. It was part psychological and part math. I hadn't looked at any math problems since college. A lot of it dealt with word problems, analyzation, and percentages. I had been good at math in the past, but I was out of practice. I got up several times during the exam and went to the bathroom. I didn't have a good feeling about it. When my time was up, I felt discouraged. Chris told me he would fax in the test, and I would know the results within twenty-four hours. But I already knew the results.

The next day, my thoughts were confirmed. I didn't pass the test. I was devasted. I was hoping that maybe I'd gotten lucky. Chris advised that I could retake the test in ninety days. I was upset and embarrassed. I had told everyone I was about to go into management. Now, they would all know I had failed the test. Furthermore, I didn't want to see Sal. I knew he would be disappointed and feel like I had wasted his time.

When I went back to work the next day, several people asked me how everything went with Chris. I was honest and told them it didn't go well. I figured there was no reason to lie about it. Of course, Sal was disappointed in me, but I didn't care. I was sick of trying to earn his approval. I decided to work my tail off and brush up on my math skills over the next three months. I couldn't wait to retake the exam.

One week shy of my ninety days, I contacted Chris again. I told him I was eager to retake the exam. He said he would be more than happy to have me take it again. He came in the next week, and I was waiting for him. I was ready to prove I could do it.

As soon as I began, my concentration heightened. I knew I was going to prove Sal wrong. I finished the test in record time and gave it to Chris, certain about all my answers. Chris told me I had more time, but I was done. He said I'd know the results the following day. Once again, I already knew the results.

The next day, Chris called me and gave me the good news. He also set me up with a phone interview for the same day with someone from our corporate office. I became nervous again because I thought after the drug test and written test, I would be done. I hadn't had to interview for a job in over five years, and this was the most important interview of my life.

A few hours later, someone called me from the corporate office and asked me ten questions. To my surprise, the questions were situational. I had encountered most of the situations as a server before. Because I had already started looking at things from the guests' perspective, it was easy to answer the questions. When the interview ended, I knew I had done well. They told me I should hear from my director the next day. I was eager.

The next day, my director called and asked me to meet at the Blue Crab later in the evening. I was glad because I had tickets to the Detroit Tigers game earlier in the day. I was grateful for the game because it calmed my nerves. I downed a couple of beers at the game, which helped ease my nerves. After the game ended, I went home to shower and change. I must've brushed my teeth about five times. I didn't want the smell of beer on me. I also picked up a pack of gum on the way to my meeting with Chris. I chewed the entire pack before I got to the Blue Crab.

As soon as I got there, Chris was already waiting for me. I was excited to hear what the next steps were. I figured I would start training in a few months.

Chris was sitting at the end of the bar, going over some things with Sal when I approached him. "Hello," I said.

Sal got up and patted me on the back. "Congrats!"

I thanked him and sat down. Chris congratulated me as well for my determination. We had small talk for a few minutes, and Chris asked me, "Are you ready?"

"Yes, I'm ready, and I'm looking forward to the next step."

"There is no next step."

I was a little confused.

"You'll begin training on Monday, and your salary will begin at $35,000."

I had no idea the pay was horrible.

"Are you okay with the offer?" he asked.

"Yes, it's fine." I was eager to begin my career.

I signed the paperwork. I was so excited! I was a manager! But I had no idea what I was getting myself into.

If I had known, I would've said hell no!

Thank you for reading *À La Carte*, the first installment in *The Restaurant Diaries*. If you enjoyed this book, please help spread the word and leave an online review. Thank you!

Stay tuned for the next installment in
The Restaurant Diaries: *The Main Course*
Coming Soon!

CONNECT WITH BRANDON D. BRADLEY
Learn more about Brandon D. Bradley and his work
www.brandondbradley.com
Connect with Brandon D. Bradley on social media
Facebook: facebook.com/brandon.bradley.9
Instagram: @Brandondbradley

www.ingramcontent.com/pod-product-compliance
Lightning Source LLC
Chambersburg PA
CBHW020329110726
47898CB00003B/804